Her shame vanished at his cool attitude

"I assume I'm to forget what happened, aren't I?" Sara flashed. "How delightful it must be to have such an expedient conscience!"

Suddenly Jude's gray eyes impaled her with a savage look. "I swear I didn't intend for things to go that far!"

"I don't suppose you did," she answered icily. "After all, there's just so much one man can do, isn't there? And you have other means of expunging your frustration."

"Would you want me to expunge it with you?" he asked smoothly. "I could, you know—and with a great amount of satisfaction."

Sara caught her breath. "For you, I suppose."

"For both of us," he told her. "And don't pretend you don't know what I mean."

ANNE MATHER
is also the author of these

Harlequin Presents

and these

Harlequin Romances

Many of these titles are available at your local bookseller.

For a free catalogue listing all available Harlequin Romances
and Harlequin Presents, send your name and address to:

HARLEQUIN READER SERVICE,
1440 South Priest Drive, Tempe, AZ 85281
Canadian address: Stratford, Ontario N5A 6W2

ANNE MATHER

duelling fire

Harlequin Books

TORONTO · LONDON · LOS ANGELES · AMSTERDAM
SYDNEY · HAMBURG · PARIS · STOCKHOLM · ATHENS · TOKYO

Harlequin Presents edition published March 1982
ISBN 0-373-10490-1

Original hardcover edition published in 1981
by Mills & Boon Limited

CHAPTER ONE

'AND are you going to accept?'

The speaker was a short plump girl, in her middle twenties, with a round good-natured face and curly dark hair. She was lounging comfortably on a couch, lazily picking the soft centres from a box of chocolates open beside her, and flicking casually through the pages of a fashion magazine.

The girl with her was her complete opposite. Tall and slim and blonde, her straight silvery hair confined at her nape with a leather thong, Sara Shelley was presently coiled on the floor, examining her profile from the lotus position. She had been sitting like that for some time now, and her friend and companion, Laura Russell, was getting tired of waiting for her reply.

'Oh, I don't know.' Sara uncoiled herself at last, and sat cross-legged looking up at her friend. 'Beggars can't be choosers, isn't that the truth? And believe me, Laura, that's what I am.'

'Rubbish!' Laura swung her feet to the floor and faced the other girl impatiently. 'You know you could always get a job here. You don't have to accept this woman's charity!'

'But it is a job, don't you see?' exclaimed Sara wryly. 'A job I'm singularly well qualified to accept. And it's all right for you to talk casually of employment, with the security of a degree behind you!'

'You're not without qualifications,' Laura protested. 'You had a good education.'

'Until I was sixteen,' Sara reminded her flatly. 'When Daddy decided I could learn more from the university of life.' She sighed. 'Not that I objected at the time.' She shook her head. 'I couldn't wait to leave school and be

5

with him. But——' Her voice broke with sudden emotion, 'how was I to know he'd walk out on me, before I was twenty-one?'

Laura's face registered her sympathy. 'Sara, he didn't walk out on you——'

'Well, what would you call it?' Sara's eyes shone with unshed tears. 'I think taking your own life is such a cowardly thing to do. Just because he believed he was a loser!'

'He did owe over thirty thousand pounds,' Laura reminded her gently. 'Oh, I'm not saying that excuses him, and abandoning you—well, I can understand how betrayed you must feel. But, darling, can you imagine how he must have felt before he—well——'

'——swallowed the overdose?' Sara completed the sentence ironically, and then got lithely to her feet, a slim tragic figure in a black track suit, her feet bare. 'Don't worry, Laura. It's two months since he died. I've come to terms with the finality of his death, and I can take it.'

Laura sighed. She felt so helpless. If only there was some way she could be of some use!

'Cheer up!' Sara was speaking again, forcing a bright smile to her generous mouth. 'Don't feel sorry for me. I don't feel sorry for myself—at least, only occasionally. And Aunt Harriet's invitation is a godsend!'

'Is it?' Laura was not so sure. 'Sara, what do you know about this woman, really know, I mean? Why, she's not even your aunt, not any real relation at all. Just a cousin of your father's.'

Sara shrugged, putting up her hands to lift the heavy weight of her hair from her shoulders. Watching her, Laura wondered if she had any idea how vulnerable she was. For twenty—almost twenty-one years—Sara had enjoyed the privilege of her father's protection, first at boarding school, and later, as Sara herself had said, accompanying him on his travels about the world. Charles Shelley had been a freelance journalist, but freelance gambler would have suited him better, Laura decided ruefully. He was good at his job, very good, but as soon as he had any money, he couldn't wait to spend it. Having known her since she was born, Laura's own mother having acted as nanny to the baby Sara, Laura felt an especial sense of responsibility for her friend, and the fact that Sara had led what many people would have regarded as a very sophisticated life seemed in no way to have equipped her for the vagaries of this world. She had always enjoyed her father's protection, he had idolised the girl—which made her lack of affectation that much more remarkable—and Laura sometimes wondered whether Charles Shelley had really intended to kill himself and leave Sara to fend for herself.

And now, out of the blue, the letter had arrived from Charles Shelley's cousin, Harriet Ferrars, sympathising with her over her father's death, and inviting her to go and live with her, as her friend and companion. Laura had never even met Harriet Ferrars. She had only rarely heard her name mentioned, and Sara herself knew nothing about the household in Wiltshire where she was expected to live. Laura found the whole idea rather suspicious, and she had lost no time in telling Sara so.

With another smile, Sara allowed her hair to tumble carelessly about her shoulders, and squatted before her friend compassionately. 'Stop worrying,' she ordered, her green eyes warm with affection. 'I haven't said I'm going yet, have I? And if I do go, and I don't like it, I can always come back. You'll take me in, won't you? You won't let me sleep on the streets.'

Laura clicked her tongue. 'Sara, be serious! You know you have a home here as long as you want one. It's a small flat, I know, but my work at the hospital keeps me out of it for long periods at a time, and if you wanted a bigger place, we could pool our resources.'

'What resources?' Sara asked teasingly, and then nodded. 'Yes, I guess we could. I wonder how much a cleaner is paid these days.'

'Sara—honestly!' Laura shook her head. 'With your looks, you could be a model.'

'A model?' Sara giggled and rose to her feet. 'Oh, Laura, I wonder if you have any idea how difficult it is to become a model! There must be dozens of hopefuls, just like me, turning up at agencies every day, and besides, I'd be no good as a model.' She grimaced. 'My breasts are too big!'

Laura pursed her lips. 'How do you know that?'

Sara ran exploratory hands down over her waist and hips. 'I just know it. Laura, they like flat-chested ladies without too many bulges——'

'You don't have bulges!'

'Perhaps not.' Sara glanced at her reflection in the convex mirror above the sideboard without approval. 'In any case, I don't see myself as a model, Laura. I'm more the cleaner type, honestly.'

Laura's lips compressed as she looked up into Sara's twinkling eyes. 'But are you the companion type?' she retorted. 'That's what you have to ask yourself. Can you honestly see yourself changing library books, or taking the poodle for a walk, or reading out loud from some ghastly romantic novel!'

'As a matter of fact, I like romantic novels,' replied Sara firmly. 'And so do you, if the contents of your bookshelf are anything to go by.'

Laura looked vaguely discomfited. 'I have to have something undemanding to read when I'm on night duty,' she defended herself, and then broke into an unwilling smile as Sara caught her eye. 'Oh, all right. So I'm a romantic, too. But do you really see yourself doing that sort of thing, week in and week out?'

'That remains to be seen,' remarked Sara lightly. 'Laura, don't be depressed. As I say, I haven't made up my mind yet. But, if nothing more exciting comes along, the least I can do is give it a whirl.'

Two weeks later, Sara began to regret those words as the jolting country train stopped at yet another junction. She had not known there were still trains like this, but Aunt Harriet's instructions had been very explicit. 'Change at Swindon,' she had written, after Sara had acknowledged and accepted her kind invitation, 'and then ask for the Buford connection. You'll be met at King's Priory, so don't worry about your luggage.'

As the train jerked on again, Sara rested her head against the shabby upholstery and rehearsed what she was going to say when Aunt Harriet asked her about her father. She was bound to ask—everyone did. And it was best to have her story intact before she reached her destination. Of course, the circumstances of Charles Shelley's demise were bound to be known to her. The papers had been full of the story. *Well-known Foreign Correspondent Found Dead*, one headline had boasted. *Drug addiction not ruled out*.

But her father had not been a drug addict, Sara comforted herself disconsolately, gazing out unseeingly at the burgeoning hedges that marched beside the track. To her knowledge, he had never taken anything stronger than aspirin, and to suggest that he had was both cruel and libellous. Nevertheless, the fact remained that he had died from an overdose of morphine, and she had been too shocked and too grief-stricken to care much what the papers said. Her father was dead, the only parent she had ever known was no longer a living breathing being, and it wasn't until after the funeral that her senses rebelled. She began to see that what he had done was unforgivable, and while it didn't stop her loving him or grieving for him, it did help to steel her against the uncertainties of the future.

Laura had been a brick, and without her uncomplicated companionship, Sara didn't know what she would have done. When she first arrived back from India, stunned and confused by her father's sudden death in

Calcutta, Laura had been the only person she could turn to, and in the weeks that followed she had earned Sara's undying gratitude. It was she who had kept the unwanted reporters at bay, who had cared for and comforted the shattered victim of Charles Shelley's suicide, and who latterly had encouraged Sara to regard the flat as her home.

But although Sara was tempted to let Laura go on looking after her, depending on her strength and letting her make all her decisions, gradually her spirit had re-asserted itself. And when Harriet Ferrars' letter arrived, she had realised that here was the opportunity to take her life into her own hands, and if she made an abysmal failure, then Laura could always say, 'I told you so'.

The train was slowing again, and Sara resignedly checked the weathered sign that teetered unreliably in the brisk April breeze. King's Priory, she read without interest, and then read it again with sudden apprehension. There was no mistake. This was the station Aunt Harriet had told her to alight at, and with a shivery sense of impatience she gathered her bags.

The carriage was almost deserted. It was one of those long cylinders, with a central passageway between rows of tables, and as there had been no one sharing her table, Sara had deposited her suitcases beneath it. She had three suitcases and an overnight bag, as well as her hand-bag and her vanity case, and although she had had Laura's help at Paddington and a porter's at Swindon, she saw with some trepidation that King's Priory did not appear to boast any labour force other than the ticket collector.

Glad that her bag and vanity case had shoulder straps, she tugged the three suitcases and the holdall to the exit, and thrust open the door just as the guard was about to blow his whistle. Obviously few passengers ever alighted at King's Priory, and he was quite prepared to send the train on its way after the briefest of stops possible.

'You ought to have been ready to get out, miss,' he grumbled testily, as she hauled her belongings down on to the platform. 'This here train has a schedule to keep to, you know. It don't wait here just for your convenience.'

Sara straightened from setting the suitcases to rights and surveyed the stout railwayman frostily. 'What you're saying, I'm sure, is that you don't run these trains for the convenience of the passengers, isn't that right?' she enquired, copying her late father's methods of intimidation.

The guard stiffened. 'There's no need to use that tone with me! Just because you nearly missed your stop——'

'I did not nearly miss my stop,' Sara contradicted him smoothly. 'However, I do have only one pair of arms, and as you can see, I have two pairs of suitcases.'

The guard muttered something under his breath, which she suspected had to do with the amount of luggage she was conveying, and then sniffed grudgingly. 'Well—no harm done,' he conceded, settling his cap more firmly on his head, and she acknowledged the faint reparation before tackling the trek to the barrier.

The man who had taken the tickets from the half dozen other commuters who had got out at King's Priory watched without expression as she transferred herself and her luggage to the gate. Then, after he had punched her ticket, he turned away, and Sara was left to make her own arrangements in the departing draught from the train.

'Thank you. Thank you so much,' she muttered broodingly to herself, as she stepped through the barrier and surveyed the empty lane beyond. There was no sign of any vehicle, other than a beaten-up wreck occupying the yard behind the stationmaster's office, and her lips tightened impatiently as she realised she didn't know what she was going to do.

Evidently, King's Priory was just a country halt, used for the most part, she suspected, by farmers and the like.

There was no pretty village street opening up beyond the station, no taxis, not even a bus stop that she could see, and her heart sank miserably at this unwelcome prospect. Aunt Harriet—or perhaps she should say *Miss* Ferrars, right now the familiar appellation seemed less than appropriate—had known what time she was due to arrive. Surely she could have ensured there was someone available to meet her, even if it was only a taxi Sara herself would have to pay for.

She sighed, and glanced back at the station. It was quite a pretty halt, she conceded reluctantly. There were anemones and violets growing among the stones that made a kind of rockery at the back of the platform, and tulips still grew between the posts of the signpost, a vivid splash of colour in the chilly air of late afternoon. If only she did not feel quite so alone, she thought with a sudden rush of misery, but she quickly quelled the unworthy feeling as purely one of self-pity.

The welcome sound of a car's engine rapidly dispelled her dejection. There was no one else waiting, and surely no other train due. The person who was driving the car had to be coming for her.

The car that eventually ground to a halt beside her was not at all the kind of vehicle Sara had expected. Used to the rather sedate tastes of her father's contemporaries, she had assumed her aunt would drive a Rover or perhaps a Volvo, or some similar kind of comfortable saloon. The sleek red Mercedes that confronted her was of the two-seater sporting variety, and even as she acknowledged this, she saw to her regret that the man levering himself from behind the wheel was far too young to be Harriet Ferrars' husband—*had she had one*! Obviously she had been mistaken in imagining this was her transport, but she couldn't help the unwilling awareness that the driver was giving her a more than cursory appraisal. Indeed, his interest bordered on the insolent, and Sara turned her long green eyes in his direction, and returned his stare with deliberate arrogance.

He really was quite something, she conceded reluctantly, even while she resented his intrusion into her life. Lean and dark and indolent, with harshly attractive features which were so much more distinctive than mere good looks, he had a lithe sinuous physique that complemented the leather jacket and tight-fitting jeans he was wearing. He was tall, too, though not angularly so, and Sara was not unaware of his powerful shoulders and the hard muscularity of his thighs.

He slammed the car door and came round the bonnet without removing his eyes from hers, and Sara's gaze faltered in the face of such blatant audacity. Just who the hell did he think he was? she asked herself indignantly, and summoned a freezing hauteur to combat his brazen effrontery.

'I guess as there's no one else around, you must be Sara Shelley,' he remarked, as she was preparing her set-down, and her jaw sagged disbelievingly. 'Is this all your luggage?' he added with a wry grimace. 'Or is the rest coming by carrier?'

Sara gathered herself abruptly. 'This is all,' she replied stiffly. 'Did—did Miss Ferrars send you? I don't believe she mentioned you.'

'She wouldn't.' The man unlocked the boot and began heaving her cases inside. 'And sure, it was Harriet who sent me. Belatedly, as you'll no doubt have gathered.'

He sounded as if he hadn't wanted to turn up here at all, and Sara could only assume he must be the son of some friend of Aunt Harriet's. Or perhaps he was another relative, she reflected thoughtfully, then coloured when she realised he had finished stowing the cases and was waiting for her to get into the car.

She was glad she was wearing trousers as she subsided into the passenger seat. At least she didn't have to worry about keeping her skirt over her knees, although she doubted that her escort was aware of the consideration.

Having disposed of the introduction, he seemed indifferent to her feelings. He had neither apologised for being late nor apprised her of his identity, and Sara resented the unspoken assumption that she should be glad that he had come at all.

The Mercedes' engine fired at the first attempt, and the sleek vehicle nosed its way out of the station yard. There were wild flowers growing in the hedges, and the faint smell of early broom in the air, and determining not to let his attitude disconcert her, Sara made an effort to be polite.

'How—how is Miss Ferrars?' she enquired, folding her hands in her lap, and as she did so, she realised how little she really knew of her father's cousin. She hardly remembered the brief occasions they had met, all of them when she was only a schoolgirl, and more interested in the dolls and icecreams than in the lady who had provided them. The visits Harriet Ferrars had made to Sara's school had been few and far between, and in the latter years she had not come at all. Her father had excused her on the grounds that 'Harriet has problems of her own,' although what those problems were he never specified. And once Sara had left St. Mawgan's, she realised shamefully, she had never even thought of 'Aunt' Harriet—until the letter arrived.

'She's okay,' her companion said now, glancing sideways at her. 'Just as autocratic as ever. Or don't you remember anything about those outings you made together?'

Sara moistened her lips. 'I—remember the cream teas.'

'Yes.' The curve of his lips was faintly derisive. 'I guess you would. Harriet always thought that everything had a price.'

Sara frowned. 'I don't know what you mean.'

He shook his head. 'It doesn't matter.' He paused. 'I guess what you want to hear is that she's looking forward to your arrival. She is.' Again that mocking twist to his mouth. 'She has great plans for you.'

Sara gazed at him somewhat resentfully. Exactly what was his relationship to Harriet Ferrars, and why should he speak so disparagingly about someone who obviously trusted him?

'You haven't told me your name, Mr—er——' she said stiffly, waiting for his insertion, and with a shrug he conceded the point.

'Jude,' he offered carelessly. 'Just Jude. You'll get used to seeing me around.'

'Will I?' Sara could not have been more surprised. Did that mean he worked for Harriet? It must. Yet she had never dreamt Harriet was affluent enough to employ anyone, much less a chauffeur. And yet what else could he be? Though he was so far removed from Sara's image of a chauffeur, it seemed almost ludicrous. How old was he? she wondered, permitting herself a fleeting assessment: twenty-eight, *thirty*? Certainly no more, and surely he was far too familiar for an employee.

'You really don't know much about Harriet, do you?' he suggested now, as the car ran between Elizabethan cottages flanking a village green. It was very pretty and picturesque, and for a moment Sara was diverted by the unexpected charm of her surroundings. But then, a challenging glance from eyes of a curious shade of light grey caused an uneasy pang of apprehension to sweep over her, and her fingers curled painfully into her palms.

'I know enough,' she declared, irritated that he should think he could speak to her in this way. 'I probably know her as well as you do. Er—how long have you been working for Miss Ferrars?'

'Working?' He gave her a mocking look. 'Let me see. Would you believe—ten years?'

'Ten years!' Sara was silenced. If he had been working for Aunt Harriet for ten years, then he probably knew she had only seen her aunt once in that time. It had been on her twelfth birthday. Her father had been covering a military take-over in some remote South American dictatorship, and she had been so pleased that someone had arrived to prove she had not been completely forgotten. Aunt Harriet had taken her out for tea, and over lemonade and cream cakes she had been the recipient of all Sara's thwarted confidences. Remembering this now, realising that this man had been working for her aunt at that time, she inwardly cringed at her own naïvety. Had Aunt Harriet relayed her confidences to him? Had her girlish chatter been the source of some amusement to them? The idea was humiliating. But then another thought struck her. Aunt Harriet had driven herself that day. She remembered distinctly. She had been driving a rather ordinary saloon car, and surely if she had had a chauffeur he would have been with her.

'I didn't know Aunt Harriet had a chauffeur,' she tendered now, realising that if this man did work for her aunt, then it was no doubt foolish to antagonise him until she saw for herself how the situation developed, and then turned bright red when he burst out laughing.

'What makes you think I'm the chauffeur?' he exclaimed, when he had sobered. 'Do I look like a chauffeur? I'm sorry, I'll have to take stock of the way I dress if I do.'

Sara pressed her lips together. 'I naturally assumed——'

'What did you naturally assume, I wonder?' Dark lashes narrowed the grey irises. 'Why should you think I was Harriet's chauffeur? What did she tell you?'

'Nothing about you, anyway,' retorted Sara hotly. 'And as to why I thought you were the chauffeur, I don't see in what other capacity you could serve my aunt.'

'Don't you? Don't you really?' His lips twisted. 'Well, don't worry about it. All will be explained in the fullness of time.'

Sara shook her head. 'I wish you'd tell me. I don't want to make any more mistakes.' She held up her head.

'I didn't realise there would be anyone else—what I mean is—I understood I was to be her companion. I thought she lived alone.'

'Harriet? Live alone?' He took his eyes from the road to stare at her incredulously. 'My God, you really don't know her, do you?'

Sara's colour refused to subside. 'Perhaps if you were a little less scathing, and a little more helpful,' she ventured.

'What? And spoil Harriet's fun? Oh, no.' He shook his head derisively. 'Well, cool it. We're almost there.'

'Are we?'

Sara's apprehensions increased as they left the village behind to plough farther into the rolling countryside. Acres of wooded hillside gave on to luscious green pastures, grazed by herds of brown and white cattle. Across the fields she could see the spire of a church, and the thatched roofs of other cottages, and here and there a white-painted farmhouse, looking totally at home in the landscape. It was a rural scene, a placid scene—but Sara's thoughts were anything but placid as she neared her destination.

'Where—where does Miss Ferrars live?' she asked, her troubled thoughts urging her into speech. 'The address was just given as Knight's Ferry, Buford, Wiltshire. What is Knight's Ferry? A village? Or the name of her house?'

'That's Knight's Ferry,' declared her companion flatly, as the road mounted a slight rise and they looked down on the turrets of a sprawling country mansion. 'Didn't you know? Harriet's father was a wealthy man, and she was his only offspring.'

'No!' Sara could not believe it. She turned bewildered eyes in his direction. 'I thought—I mean, I assumed——'

'—that she was some lonely old lady, in need of your care and protection?' he finished for her drily. 'Nothing could be farther from the truth.'

Sara shook her head and turned to look at the house

again, but they were on the downward slope, and tall
hedges obscured the view. All she could see was another
house in the distance, standing on a knoll, which made it
visible from the road. A larger house, she estimated,
backed by an imposing sweep of firs, and with acres of
parkland falling away to where she guessed her aunt's
house was situated.

She caught her breath, and her companion, misinterpreting her reaction, said cynically: 'Yes, impressive,
isn't it? Linden Court.' He paused. 'Lord Hadley's resi-
dence.'

'Is it?' Sara's voice revealed her uncertainty, and as if
taking pity on her, his eyes darkened with unexpected
sympathy.

'Poor Sara,' he said, and her indignation at his casual
use of her Christian name was superseded by other, more
disturbing emotions. 'You really don't know what you're
letting yourself in for, do you? Just don't let Harriet eat
you alive!'

CHAPTER TWO

ANY response Sara might have made to this remark was
thwarted by the sudden eruption of a horse and rider into
the road in front of them. It all happened so quickly,
Sara was full of admiration for her companion's swift
reactions as he stood on his brakes. The Mercedes swerved
only slightly, the tyres squealing on the gravelly surface,
and they halted abruptly only a few feet from the animal's
rearing hooves.

'Bloody fool!' Jude muttered savagely, thrusting open
his door, and as he did so the rider swung down from his
sweating mount to confront him.

Sara found that she was shaking, too, but she watched

with some trepidation as the two men faced one another with apparent recognition. They were not at all alike, she acknowledged inconsequently. The man Jude was so dark and aggressive, the other man mousey-fair and conciliatory. It was obvious in the way he held up his hand in mitigation, and the disarming smile of apology that split his gentler features.

'I'm most awfully sorry, Jude,' Sara heard him say contritely, soothing the fretful horse with his hand on its muzzle. 'I had no idea you'd be coming along here right at this moment. Juniper wanted to take the hedge, and dammit, I just let him.'

Jude shook his head impatiently, but he was evidently mollified by the other man's attitude. 'You'll kill yourself one of these days, Rupert,' he declared roughly. 'This may be a quiet road, but it's not a private one, and I don't think your father would approve of being presented with a bill for a new Mercedes, do you?'

'Heavens, no!' the young man grimaced. 'Pater and I are not exactly on the best of terms as it is, right now, and Juniper breaking a leg would be the last straw!'

'Yes, well——' Jude's expression was not incomprehensible, Sara thought, bearing in mind that the horse was not his concern. 'So long as we understand one another, hmm? I wouldn't want Harriet upset.'

'Lord, no,' the young man chuckled, and watching them Sara wondered what kind of a relationship two such opposites could have. That they knew one another very well was obvious. What was less obvious was what they might have in common.

As if becoming aware that they had an audience, the fair man suddenly turned and looked in her direction, and Sara pressed her shoulders back in the seat and endeavoured not to notice. But to her astonishment Jude, observing the other man's interest, invited him casually to come and meet her.

'This is Sara Shelley,' he said, introducing them

through the open window of the car. 'Sara, this is Rupert Hadley, Lord Hadley's son.'

Once again his use of her name went unremarked beneath Sara's astonishment at the introduction. This was Lord Hadley's son! The son of the owner of that magnificent stately home on the hill! She could hardly believe it, and while all her instincts urged her to get out of the car to speak to him, Jude's indolent stance against the door prevented her. How on earth could an employee of her aunt's be familiar with the son of one of England's aristocracy? It didn't make sense, unless her assessment of the situation was lacking some vital clue.

'So pleased to meet you, Miss Shelley.'

Rupert Hadley had put his hand through the window, and with a feeling of disbelief Sara offered her own. His hand, despite his hard riding, was quite soft, and she guessed the leather gauntlets he wore protected his skin from any abrasion.

'How do you do?' she responded politely, not quite knowing how she ought to address him, and his lips parted broadly to reveal uneven white teeth.

'Are you staying with Miss Ferrars?' he enquired, making no move to go, but before Sara could reply, Jude interposed for her.

'Sara is Harriet's niece,' he declared, his grey eyes challenging her to contradict him. 'She's—er—she's come to stay with us for a while. Her father died recently, and Harriet's her only relation.'

'I see.' Rupert Hadley was evidently intrigued by the combination of silvery-tipped lashes and long green eyes, but as if he was in charge of the situation, Jude chose to break up the gathering.

'We must be going,' he said, walking round the car to slide in beside Sara again, and she stiffened instinctively when he leant half across her to make his farewells to the other man. 'See you later, Rupert,' he remarked, and Sara was aware again of a certain proprietorial note in his voice. But the brushing of his shoulder against her arm and the lean hardness of his thigh pressed briefly against hers during the exchange robbed her of any other speculations.

Rupert Hadley watched them go, a rather stolid figure in his tweed hacking jacket and fawn breeches. He didn't wear a hat, Sara noticed, and his fair hair lifted slightly in the breeze as they passed. But it was not this that caused her to look back over her shoulder. It was the sudden uncanny feeling that she had seen his face before, and she was still giving this consideration when they turned between stone gateposts and negotiated the narrow drive which led to the forecourt in front of the house.

Knight's Ferry had probably originally gained its name from the fact that the River Rowan glinted in the late afternoon sunlight only a dozen yards from its doors. Sara guessed there had once been a ferry to cross the wide stretch of calm water, but no doubt time, and the erection of bridges, had robbed it of any usage. Still, she could not deny a surge of pleasure as she looked at the mellowed old building, with its ivy-covered walls and leaded dormer windows, the turrets she had seen earlier like some medieval reminder of the days when fortification was a way of life. The house belonged to no particular period that she could identify, and she surmised it had been added to over the years. Now it sprawled like a matron gone to seed, large and comfortable, but lacking in elegance.

Sara was admiring the gardens when the door to the house opened, and a woman appeared at the head of a short flight of steps. Immediately, her momentary sense of reprieve was over, and she turned her attention to where Jude was unloading her suitcases, silently begging for his intercession.

'Sara! Sara, my child! How good it is to see you after all this time!' Harriet Ferrars' words were warming and disarming, and Sara's gaze was drawn back to her as the woman advanced towards her.

Her memories of Aunt Harriet were vague, and in her brief experience people generally aged quicker than memory allowed. That was why, although she knew the woman could not be much more than fifty, she had expected someone who looked middle-aged and matronly, a little like the house, she mused, struck by the simple comparison.

But Harriet Ferrars did not look middle-aged or matronly. Indeed, if Sara had not known the truth, she would have estimated her age to be somewhere in her thirties, and that only because of her carriage and maturity. Her face and figure were those of a much younger woman. Her skin was virtually unlined, and the two-piece suit she was wearing, in dusky blue silk jersey, accentuated the slender line of her hips and the shapely length of her legs. Her make-up was faultless, her hair, a rich chestnut brown, worn in a loose casual style. She was little like the girl's image of her, and Sara knew a moment's trepidation for the things that Jude had told her.

Then she was embraced with genuine affection, the kisses that were delivered on both cheeks leaving a delicate fragrance of Eau de Lancome behind them. 'Sara,' Harriet said again, drawing back and shaking her head. 'My dear, you are simply delightful!'

Sara coloured, as much from the knowledge that Jude was watching them and could hear every word as from any embarrassment at the effusive comment.

'Thank you,' she murmured, forcing a smile. And then: 'It's good to see you again, too, Aunt Harriet.'

'Yes.' Harriet held her at arm's length for a moment, surveying her with a thoroughness Sara found quite disconcerting. But after a moment her aunt released her, and tucked a confiding hand through her arm.

'I was so sorry to hear about your father, my dear,' she said, broaching the subject Sara least wanted to talk about. 'It must have been a terrible shock for you. That's why I sent for you. One needs relatives at a time like this.'

'Shall I put the cases in the rose room?' asked Jude, interrupting them, and Harriet glanced round at him with a barely perceptible tightening of her lips.

'You know as well as I do that that's the room I've chosen for Sara,' she declared, an edge to her voice, and Jude shrugged his shoulders rather mockingly as he bent to pick up the luggage.

'Come along, dear.' Harriet patted Sara's hand and urged her towards the house. 'It's still cold, despite the sunshine. But I think you'll find you'll be comfortable here.'

'I'm sure I shall.' Sara wanted to say something, some words of gratitude, but it was difficult with Jude's sardonic presence right behind them, and she waited until they had entered the spacious entrance hall before offering her awkward thanks.

'My dear, don't think of it.' Harriet cast a thoughtful glance at Jude's back as he strode vigorously up the stairs with two of the cases, and then gestured towards a door across the hall. 'Come along. We'll have tea in here. I told Janet to make it, as soon as I heard the car.'

Sara looked about her in some bemusement as they crossed the hall and entered a warm, attractive sitting room. Whereas the hall had been oak-panelled and a little dark, despite the rich red pile of the carpet, the room Harriet showed her into was light and airy, with long french doors that opened on to the garden at the back of the house. A low stone balustrade surrounded a flagged terrace, which in turn gave on to the gardens, and beyond them, the river.

The room itself was decorated in a bright, cheerful style, with chintz-covered armchairs and a long sofa. There were cabinets against the walls, housing a variety of china and ornaments, a kneehole desk liberally covered with papers, and bookshelves flanking the open fireplace, where a real log fire spluttered in the grate.

Harriet closed the door and then looked happily at

her guest. 'There now,' she said. 'Isn't this cosy? Come along, take off your coat. I'm sure you won't need it in here.'

Sara was sure, too. As well as the open fire, there were also radiators, and she guessed the crackling logs were just an attractive adjunct to the real heating system. Smiling, she unfastened the buttons of the warm suede jacket she had worn with corded pants, and revealed the cream woollen jersey she had worn underneath.

Harriet helped her off with her jacket, dropping it carelessly over the back of a chair before gesturing that Sara should take one of the armchairs that faced one another across the hearth. Sara did as she suggested, holding out her cold hands to the blaze, and Harriet came to sit opposite, smiling her satisfaction.

'So, Sara,' she said, resting her arms along the arms of the chair, long fingers with painted nails hanging over the end. 'How was your journey? Not too arduous, I hope. Trains can be so unreliable, and whenever possible I use the car.'

'It was all right.' Sara spoke rather nervously. 'The trains were quite punctual, actually.'

'But we were not, is that what you're saying?' asked Harriet perceptively. 'My dear, you must blame me. I simply wasn't ready.'

'Oh, no.' Sara had no wish that Aunt Harriet should think her words were meant as a criticism. 'I mean—I'd only been there about five minutes when Mr—er—Mr Jude arrived. I—I was very grateful to see him.'

'Were you?' Harriet's lips tightened once more, as they had done outside, but she made no comment about her chauffeur. *Only he wasn't her chauffeur*, Sara reminded herself tensely, realising she had still not discovered his real designation.

A tap at the door heralded the arrival of the maid with the tea. An elderly woman, with dour Scots features, wheeled a laden trolley across the patterned carpet, and set it firmly in front of her mistress.

'This is Janet,' Harriet announced, smiling up at the woman disarmingly. 'Janet, this is my niece, Sara Shelley. Isn't she lovely?'

If Sara was embarrassed by her method of introduction, Janet seemed unaware of it. 'Pleased to meet you, miss,' she declared, her tone belying the greeting, and in an accent unimpaired by however long she had lived in England. Then, without waiting for any response, she marched out of the room again, leaving Sara with the distinct impression that she did not approve.

'Don't mind Janet,' Harriet said quickly, drawing the trolley towards her and taking charge of the teapot. 'She's been with me too long, I'm afraid, and familiarity breeds contempt, don't they say?' She smiled, and resumed setting out the teacups. 'Now, what will you have? Cream and sugar? Or are you like me, and prefer your tea with lemon?'

'Just cream, please.' Sara had never acquired a taste for English tea served with lemon. No matter what the country of its origin, it did not taste like the tea she and her father used to enjoy in Nagpur, or perhaps it was the surroundings that made that drink so distinctive.

The trolley also had plates of small sandwiches, scones and a rich madeira cake, and a variety of biscuits. Sara reflected, as she munched a smoked salmon sandwich, that anyone with a weight problem would have to be careful here, and although she had never been troubled that way, she had never treated food as a ritual before. Except when Aunt Harriet had taken her out to tea, she amended, brushing a crumb from her lips, as visions of thick clotted cream and Cornish strawberry jam floated before her eyes.

As she took another sandwich she wondered apprehensively if the man Jude would join them for tea. His attitude had been quite familiar, but there were only two cups, and as the minutes stretched Sara started to relax.

'You were in India when it happened, weren't you?' Harriet said, after pouring herself a second cup of tea. She looked at Sara sympathetically. 'You don't mind me asking, do you, dear? Only I think it's best if we get it out of the way first, don't you?'

'Right.' Sara nodded. 'Yes. We were in Calcutta, actually.' Her throat tightened. 'He was covering the elections.'

'So I heard.' Harriet's tongue appeared, to moisten her upper lip. 'It must have been terrible for you—not knowing anyone, not knowing the language . . .'

'Oh, I knew people.' Sara steeled herself to talk of it. 'We had a number of friends there. And I knew a little of the language. We'd been there before, you see.'

'Yes, but——' Harriet sought for words, 'it's not like your own country, is it? Not like England.'

'As a matter of fact, I was glad,' Sara confessed huskily. 'The formalities were over so much sooner there. They have to be. The climate, you know——'

'Of course.'

'As soon as the cause of death had been disclosed—they conducted a post-mortem, you see—the—the body—had to be disposed of. I chose cremation. It was what he would have wanted.'

'My child, how awful for you! Having a funeral without any mourners!'

Sara shook her head. 'There were mourners. The—the officials who—who knew him, and other press men——'

'All the same——' Harriet sighed. 'There was no question of bringing his body back to England, I suppose?'

Sara pressed her lips together for a moment. 'I don't think he would have wanted that. He—he never regarded England as his home, not really. He was a nomad.' She took a deep breath. 'I think he probably subscribed to the theory that his life was like the arc of an arrow. He wanted to remain where it rested.'

Harriet nodded. 'What can I say? You knew him so

much better than anyone else. It had to be your decision.'

'Yes.'

Sara sighed, and with a characteristic lift of her slim shoulders, Harriet shrugged the unpleasant topic aside. 'Enough of that,' she declared, and Sara was relieved she had not had to explain the circumstances of Charles Shelley's death. For the present at least her aunt was prepared to let sleeping dogs lie, and Sara knew a sense of gratitude for her tact and understanding. Remembering what Jude had said about Aunt Harriet, she also felt a kindling of resentment. For whatever purpose, he had tried to influence her against her aunt, and she despised his reasons for doing so. He had almost succeeded in convincing her that her own opinion of Miss Ferrars was faulty, and that the only reason Harriet had for bringing her here was to satisfy some motive of her own.

'So tell me,' her aunt was continuing, 'what have you been doing with yourself since you got back to England? You wrote that you'd been living with a friend. Did you find a job?'

'I'm afraid not,' Sara grimaced, glad to be back on firm ground again. 'Jobs aren't that easy to come by, especially for someone like me, with practically no qualifications.'

'No, you're right.' Harriet lifted her cup and saucer and leaned back comfortably in her chair, folding her legs in such a way that the side vents in her skirt exposed a considerable length of thigh. 'So you were quite relieved to get my invitation? I haven't dragged you away from any exciting career in London?'

'Heavens, no!' Sara's mouth curved upward. 'And I was pleased when you wrote to me. Although whether I'll be suitable for the position you mentioned is something we'll both have to find out.'

'Oh, you'll be suitable, won't she, Harriet?'

The hateful taunting voice of the man who had driven

her from the station suspended their conversation, and glancing round Sara saw him, propped idolently against the frame of the door. He, too, had discarded his leather jerkin to reveal a close-fitting navy silk shirt, and as she watched he straightened away from the door and sauntered confidently into the room.

'Really, Jude, I wish you'd knock!' exclaimed Harriet tersely, casting a half apologetic smile in Sara's direction. 'If you want some tea, you'll have to get a cup. Janet didn't expect us to be interrupted.'

'No, ma'am. I see, ma'am. Sorry, to be sure, ma'am. But I've taken the miss's cases to her room, and I wondered if there'd be anything else, ma'am!'

'Really, Jude, you're not very funny!' Harriet's expression mirrored her exasperation, but instead of ordering him out of the room as Sara had expected, she expelled her breath shortly, and resumed drinking her tea.

Jude stood between the chairs, his hands pushed carelessly into the low belt of his jeans. He exuded an air of raw masculinity in that essentially feminine room, and Sara, much as she would like to, could not quite forget it.

She cast a hasty glance up at him, only to find he was looking at Aunt Harriet, and Sara's cheeks suddenly burned at the insolent manner of that appraisal. He was looking at her as if—as if—Sara's mind could go no further. But she wished with all her might that Aunt Harriet would pull her skirt back over her knees.

'Where were we?'

Harriet's encouraging words brought Sara up with a start, and she clattered her cup noisily as she set it down on the trolley. 'You—er—you were about to tell me what my duties will be,' she prompted, trying to ignore their unwelcome visitor, and then looked up with irritation when he smothered a stifled laugh.

'Jude, if you have nothing better to do than stand here, making a fool of me, I wish you would leave,' Harriet declared, mildly Sara thought. 'Don't you have anything useful to accomplish? Like—changing for dinner, for example!'

'*Touché!*' Jude's harsh mouth softened into irony. 'Okay, Harriet, I'll leave you to—instruct our guest in her—duties.' He paused. 'You might be interested to know, however, that she met the heir this afternoon.'

Sara blinked. What did he mean? She met the air? It didn't make sense. But Harriet was looking up at him now with scarcely concealed agitation.

'What do you mean?' she exclaimed. 'Jude, what have you done? How could she—how could *Sara* have met anyone between here and the station?'

Jude rocked back on his booted heels. 'Hadley almost straddled the bonnet of the car,' he remarked indifferently, and Sara realised he was referring to the accident they had almost had. 'Crazy young idiot! He could have killed us all.'

'Might I remind you, that "crazy young idiot" is only eight months younger than you, Jude,' Harriet retorted. Then she turned back to Sara. 'What did you think of Rupert, my dear? A handsome young man, isn't he?'

'He seemed very nice,' Sara conceded, a little awkwardly, and Harriet nodded her agreement.

'He is. He's a little wild, of course, a little reckless, perhaps. But charming, nonetheless.'

'Not to mention the fact that he's heir to his father's fortune,' inserted Jude drily, and Sara suddenly realised what his earlier statement had meant. Not air, but *heir*. She had met the heir that afternoon.

Harriet ignored Jude's mocking comment, and offered Sara more tea. 'I—er—I've known Rupert's father for a number of years,' she said. 'Lord Hadley, you know. This house was once part of the Hadley estate. You may have noticed Linden Court on your way here.'

Sara glanced awkwardly up at Jude, then she nodded. 'Yes. Yes, I did,' she confirmed. 'It looks a beautiful building.'

'It is.' Harriet's mouth curved, whether reminiscently or not Sara couldn't quite judge, but for a few moments she was silent, thinking. 'I've always loved it. Ever since my father bought Knight's Ferry.'

'More than three decades ago,' inserted Jude flatly, bringing Harriet's eyes back to him. 'You'll excuse me, I'm sure, if I go and check on Midnight. Unlike the rest of us, she can't call for help.'

When the door had closed behind him Sara expected her aunt to make some explanation for his conduct, but she didn't. Apart from offering the information that Midnight was a mare who was presently in foal, Harriet said no more about him, returning instead to Sara's reasons for coming to stay with her.

'I think we should show you your room first,' she declared getting to her feet, and Sara copied her. 'After all, we want you to be happy here, and you can't possibly decide that you want to stay, before you've even looked over the house.'

'I'm sure it will be perfect,' protested Sara, picking up her jacket and her handbag as she followed her aunt out of the room. 'Honestly, Aunt Harriet, I'm so grateful to you for inviting me. Where I sleep is of little importance.'

'Oh, you're wrong.' Harriet turned to smile at her as they began to mount the carpeted stairs. 'And my dear, would you think me horribly conceited if I asked you not to call me *Aunt* Harriet? I mean,' she hastened on rather apologetically, 'when you were a little girl—well, it was a token of respect. But now we're both grown-ups, your calling me aunt does seem rather silly, don't you think?

Sara lifted her shoulders. 'Whatever you say.'

'You don't mind?' Harriet was endearingly anxious, and Sara shook her head.

'Of course not. Why should I mind? After all, it isn't as if you are my aunt really.'

'That's what I thought.' Harriet looked pleased. 'So,

it's just plain old Harriet from now on, hmm?'

'Harriet,' Sara agreed, realising that no one else would describe her father's cousin as either plain or old.

The staircase curved in a graceful arc to the gallery above. A railed balustrade overlooked the hall below, and wall sconces illuminated several white panelled doors and two corridors leading in opposite directions, to the separate wings of the house.

'This is my room,' Harriet declared, indicating a door near the head of the stairs. 'I've put you in the rose room, which is along here. It's quite a pretty apartment, so I hope you like it.'

They walked along the corridor which lay to the left of the gallery. It was a wide corridor with a number of doors opening from it, and a long window at the end which allowed shafts of evening sunlight to stripe the dark red carpet. Harriet stopped at one of the doors and thrust it open, then preceded Sara into the room, switching on the lamps.

Sara's first impression was of a comfortable sitting room, set with a desk and armchairs, and even a table for taking meals, if she chose. But as her eyes surveyed the room she saw that the living area was only half the apartment. A wide archway and two shallow steps gave access to the sleeping compartment, where a square four-poster bed was daintily hung with chiffon drapes. Everything—the carpet, the silk curtains at the windows, the drapes above the bed, even the patterned quilt itself—was tinted a delicate shade of pink, and Sara had no need to wonder why this was called the rose room.

'The bathroom's through here, of course,' declared Harriet, mounting the two steps and indicating a door at the far side of the bedroom. 'Well, what do you think? Do you like it?'

'Who wouldn't?' Sara was bemused. It was so vastly different from the austere little room she had expected. 'You really oughtn't to have gone to so much trouble.'

'Trouble? Trouble? It was no trouble, my dear.' Harriet came down the steps again, and with a surge of sudden gratitude Sara hugged her. 'Really,' she averred, with what the girl felt was genuine sincerity. 'It's the least I could do for dear Charles's orphaned daughter.'

Sara sighed. 'But you hardly saw us,' she exclaimed, guiltily aware of their neglect. 'Harriet, I don't know how I'm going to be able to repay you.'

'Oh, we'll find a way,' declared Harriet, squeezing her shoulder warmly. 'And now I must go and check that everything's organised for dinner, or your opinion of our hospitality will suffer a distinct setback.'

Left to herself, Sara wandered about the apartment. Her suitcases, she saw, had been deposited on the ottoman at the foot of the bed, and her step faltered a moment as she thought of the man who had brought her here. The relationship he had with Harriet was certainly a strange one, and she pushed aside the unwilling suspicion that it was more than that of employer and employee. After all, Jude had worked for her aunt for ten years. He had said so. And the familiarity of their association could well be the result. But what did he do? What was his designation? And why should it matter to her, when she was unlikely to have anything to do with him?

There was a ready supply of writing paper and envelopes in the desk, and Sara decided she would write to Laura this evening. The older girl had been much concerned about her decision to accept Harriet's invitation, and it would be a relief to her to know that everything had turned out so well. Indeed, Sara doubted she would believe that such a fairy godmother still existed, and she was looking forward to describing the house to her, and this room which was so delightful.

There was plenty of hanging space in the long fitted closets, and realising she was probably expected to change for dinner, too, Sara hastily rescued her keys and unlocked her suitcases. The drawers of the dressing table and a squat little chest took all her underclothes and nightwear, and there were lots of hangers to take her suits and dresses.

One of the suitcases and the holdall contained her personal possessions. These were treasured mementoes and photographs, newspaper cuttings of her father's, the silver-backed brushes he had bought her on her eighteenth birthday, and the books she had collected over the years. She stood a framed picture of her father on the dressing table, and set out the silver-backed brushes, and as she did so, she reflected how little she had to remind her of the man who had had such an influence on her life.

The evening shadows were falling by the time she had unpacked her belongings and taken a quick shower. The bathroom adjoining the bedroom was just as charming as the rest of the apartment, and Sara had taken pleasure in the cream tiles, each displaying a pink rosebud, and the rose-tinted bath, that was sunk into the floor. She showered in the fluted perspex cubicle, taking care to keep her hair dry, and then padded back into the bedroom to decide what she should wear.

A simple black dress seemed appropriate, and would equip her for any occasion. Until she knew what the routine was at Knight's Ferry, it was safer to follow her instincts, and the dress she chose was plain, but exquisitely cut. Her father had bought it for her, in one of his more extravagant moods. They had been staying in Monte Carlo, and he had had a good win at the Casino—or so he had said. Since then, Sara had learned that Charles Shelley had seldom been out of debt, but like all gamblers he enjoyed spending money, and he was never mean when he was in funds.

Before putting on the dress, Sara gave some consideration to her make-up. A plum-coloured eyeshadow toned with a deeper-tinted lip-gloss, while a touch of mascara darkened the silvery tips of her lashes. Her make-up was light but subtle, and in no way compared to Harriet's immaculate appearance, which must have taken her hours to apply. Nevertheless, the result had been startling, and Sara wondered whether that was why her aunt had been late.

Her hair offered no problems. It was straight and silky; she brushed it until it shone, and then confined it again at her nape, this time with an ivory clasp.

The dress slid easily over her hips, caressing her skin sensuously. Although it was made of some manufactured fabric, it had the feel of silk, the dipping cowl neckline exposing the curve of her throat. Wide sleeves were drawn from a loosely draped bodice, and the wrap-around skirt opened from waist to hem. Fortunately, the generous cut of the overlap prevented any immodest display.

The little carriage clock on the mantel chimed the half hour as she was adjusting the strap of her shoe, and she caught her breath. Seven-thirty, she thought, with some trepidation. And Harriet had said dinner was usually served about eight.

Realising she would have to go down, Sara cast another glance at her appearance. Did she look all right? Was her lipstick smudged? An anxious finger discovered it was only a shadow cast by the lamp beside her bed, and she relaxed. Heavens, why was she so nervous? What had she to be afraid of?

Shrugging impatiently, she decided she would have to go. This was no time to have second thoughts, to wonder whether she had done the right thing. And besides, it was all so much different from what she had anticipated. Harriet was charming, her house was delightful, and she was going to be happy here.

Thrusting her fears aside, she opened the door and stepped into the corridor. Someone had turned on the lights, and the corridor glowed in the artificial illumination cast from beneath bronze shades. Its mellow patina gleamed on brass and polished wood, and as she descended the stairs she was struck by the simple elegance of the hall below. Now that a glittering chandelier had been lit, the panelling had a rich, lustrous sheen, and its earlier, gloomy appearance was quite dispelled by a huge bowl of spring flowers resting on an old-fashioned umbrella stand. There was a semi-circular table, with an oval silver tray— *for letters?*—Sara wondered musingly, and a little velvet armchair with curly wooden arms, set beside the little stand that held the telephone.

Reaching the bottom of the stairs, Sara was uncertain where she should go. Harriet had only shown her the small sitting room, and she was looking about her doubtfully when a door behind her opened and the man Jude appeared.

He evidently intended eating dinner with them, she thought, viewing the dark trousers and fine suede jacket he was wearing. Even his brown silk shirt had a lace jabot, though he wore no tie, the strong column of his throat dark against the fabric. His dark hair had been smoothly combed and lay thick against his head, with only the merest fraction overlapping his collar at the back.

His appraisal of her was no less comprehensive, she realised, flushing as he detected her eyes upon him. 'Well, well, Miss Shelley,' he remarked sardonically, propping one hand against the jamb. 'You look lost. Can I help you?'

'I—I was looking for Harr—for Miss Ferrars,' she admitted reluctantly. 'Do you know where she is?'

'Still dressing, I should think,' he answered, moving his shoulders in a dismissing gesture. 'Come and have a drink with me.' He nodded to the room behind him. 'We usually foregather in here.'

'Oh—very well.' Sara wasn't enthusiastic, but there wasn't much else she could do, so she crossed the floor towards him, stiffening as he stood aside to let her pass, and she smelt the faint aroma of Scotch on his breath.

'Why do I get the impression your name should be Lamb, not Shelley?' he remarked lazily, and she cast an indignant look up at him.

'Lady Caroline Lamb was associated with Byron, not Shelley,' she retorted, pleased to have thwarted him, but he was not finished.

'I might have been referring to Mary Shelley,' he pointed out drily, his grey eyes showing amusement. 'But actually, I wasn't even thinking of them.'

Sara was confused, and showed it. 'Mr Jude——'

'Just Jude,' he corrected. 'And before you ask, it was a quotation from Isaiah I was referring to. Now, shall we have that drink?'

CHAPTER THREE

Sara saw that she was in what appeared to be a library. There were bookshelves from floor to ceiling on three walls and a desk, set beneath long windows, on the fourth. An open fire broke up one wall of shelves, and as it was getting dark outside, it was reflected in the window panes, warm and inviting.

But Sara was scarcely aware of her surroundings. She was still puzzling what Jude had said to her, and it irritated her anew that he apparently had the knack of disconcerting everyone who came into contact with him.

'What will you have? Sherry? Gin? Whisky?'

Her brooding introspection was interrupted by that lazily attractive voice, and she turned to find him examining the bottles contained in a small cabinet.

'Do you have—Martini?' she asked, choosing something innocuous, and his mouth turned down wryly as he completed his inspection.

'Only vodka and Pernod,' he told her without contrition. 'Let me make you a cocktail. I do quite a passable Screwdriver.'

'Sherry,' declared Sara firmly, deciding she needed to keep her wits about her, and she watched him reluctantly as he filled her glass.

'So—what do you think of us?' he enquired, retrieving his glass, which contained the Scotch she had detected earlier. 'Not quite what you expected, I imagine. Bearing in mind what you told me earlier.'

'I wish you'd forget what I told you earlier,' Sara retorted. 'I—I was nervous then. It was a long time since I'd last seen Aunt—I mean, Harriet. Now that I've got to know her again, I realise how immature I must have sounded.'

'I imagine anyone over the age of thirty would appear quite ancient to a schoolgirl,' Jude remarked, propping himself against the bookshelves. 'Won't you sit down?'

He gestured towards a leather sofa set to one side of the fireplace, but Sara gave an involuntary shake of her head. She felt more capable of facing him on her two feet, and besides, she resented his arbitrary assumption of the role of host. It lent weight to her suspicion that his position at Knight's Ferry was not a straightforward one, and the less pleasant aspects of this conclusion were not something she wanted to contemplate right now.

'Tell me,' she said, with great daring she thought, 'what exactly do you do, Mr—er—Jude? My aunt—that is, Harriet—mentioned something about—horses?'

Jude's mouth compressed. 'Midnight? The mare?' He shrugged. 'She hasn't foaled yet, if that's what you mean.'

Sara moistened her upper lip. 'That wasn't ex-actly——'

'Oh, I see.' His expression hardened. 'You mean am I the stable hand?' He finished the whisky in his glass. 'Without wanting to disappoint you, no. That is not my primary function.'

Sara cradled her glass between her palms. The obvious rejoinder to this was beyond her ability, so instead she said, rather weakly: 'Does Miss Ferrars have many horses?'

'One or two,' he replied after a moment, moving away from the bookshelves to fix himself another drink. 'Five, to be precise. Why? Do you like horses? Do you ride?'

'I have—ridden, yes.' Sara was tentative. 'Mostly abroad. Nothing very startling, I'm afraid.'

'But you do like it? Riding, I mean?'

Sara shrugged. 'Quite.' She was reluctant. 'Why? Does Harriet?'

'Harriet?' Jude put the stopper back into the whisky decanter and surveyed her mockingly. 'I doubt if Harriet's ever swung her leg across a saddle,' he replied rather crudely. 'Outdoor sports are not her scene.'

Sara pressed her lips together. So why had he asked her? she wondered impatiently. Surely he didn't imagine she might consider riding with him. His arrogance was equal to it, and her eyes flashed fire as she met his cynical gaze.

'You know Harriet very well, don't you, Mr Jude?' she declared with grim temerity. 'I wonder if she realises how outspoken you are on her behalf.'

Jude laughed then, a faintly derisive laugh that brought the hot colour to her cheeks. 'Oh, I think she might,' he retorted, with gentle irony, and the door behind him opened before Sara could ask him what he meant.

Harriet's appearance made Sara realise how conservative her own choice of dress had been. This evening, the older woman was wearing bronze tapered pants and a glittering sequinned jacket, with a wealth of chunky jewellery dispersed about her person. Her heels were higher than any Sara would dare to wear, but she moved easily, faltering only momentarily when her gaze met that of Jude.

'Oh, you're here,' she murmured, her fingertips brushing almost absently over his sleeve. Then she caught sight of Sara and withdrew her hand. 'My dear, how lovely you look! Doesn't she, Jude?' She turned to the man with

a strange expression, almost daring him to contradict her.
'Don't you think Sara looks delightful?'

'I think the word is irresistible,' remarked Jude obscurely, and Sara wished she could combat his mocking
insolence. But Harriet took no offence at his ironic tone,
and accepted the drink he proffered her with contem-
plative abstraction.

'It seems a shame to waste it all on a family dinner,'
she remarked, tucking her arm through Sara's. 'But tomorrow evening I've arranged a little party, so we can
look forward to that.'

'Oh, really . . .' Sara moved her shoulders in some
embarrassment. 'You don't have to worry about me,
Aunt—I mean, Harriet.' She flushed again at the careless
error. 'I didn't come here to—to be entertained. I just
want to earn my keep in any way I can.'

'You will,' remarked Jude drily, swallowing the rest of
his drink in an impatient gulp, and setting the glass down
on the tray. 'Well, I must be going, ladies. Forgive my
abrupt departure, Sara, but it may reassure you not to
have to eat dinner with the hired help!'

Sara was embarrassed, but fortunately Harriet's reaction overrode her involuntary denial. 'Jude, you're not
going out tonight!' It was a cry of frustration, made the
more so by Harriet's relinquishing Sara's arm to grasp that
of the man.

'I'm afraid so.' Jude was firm, and he removed Harriet's
clinging fingers from his sleeve with cool deliberation.

Harriet sucked in her breath. 'You're taking the girl
out?' she exclaimed angrily, and Jude inclined his head as
he combed back an unruly swathe of dark hair with impatient fingers.

'Why not? She enjoys my company,' he confirmed, evidently immune to her disapproval, and Sara, briefly
meeting the hardness of those curiously light eyes, wished
herself far from this room and its discomfiting revelations.

'Does she?' Harriet's response was contemptuous, but

with a great effort of will she managed to control the
impulse to say any more. With her fingers locked tightly
together, she gave him silent permission to leave them,
and Jude cast Sara a mocking glance as he let himself
indolently out of the room.

Alone, the two women exchanged awkward smiles. Sara
was embarrassed at having witnessed such a scene, and
Harriet seemed absorbed with her thoughts, and less than
willing to share them. If only she knew Harriet well
enough to offer some advice, Sara thought indignantly,
her earlier sense of repugnance giving way to compassion.
If what she suspected was true, and Harriet did nurture
some affection for the young man, she ought to be warned
of his insolence and his disloyalty, for whatever else could
one call his overbearing arrogance?

'Harriet——'

'Sara——'.

They both started to speak, and then broke off together
in the same way. Sara, half glad that she had not been
allowed to finish what she had started, insisted that
Harriet have her say, and the older woman patted her
arm before putting down her glass.

'I just wanted to say you mustn't take my arguments
with Jude seriously,' she said. 'He and I—well, we've
known one another a long time, and sometimes—sometimes, I'm afraid, I allow familiarity to get the better of
me.'

Sara was taken aback. 'Honestly, Harriet, you don't
have to explain yourself to me——'

'Oh, but I do.' Harriet was quite recovered from her
upset now. 'I mean, I wouldn't want you to think that
Jude and I don't—understand one another.'

'Really, Harriet——'

'Jude's a little wild sometimes, that's all,' the older
woman carried on, almost as if Sara hadn't spoken. 'He
likes to show his independence. That's natural. We all
like to show our independence sometimes, don't we?'

Sara shook her head. 'It's nothing to do with me.'

'Oh, but it is.' Harriet hesitated for a moment, and then, as if having second thoughts, poured herself another drink. 'After all, you're going to be living here—for a while at least—and so is Jude. I don't want you to—well, take sides.'

The qualification of Harriet's comment did not register right then. What did was the information that Jude actually lived here, in the house. But where? And how? And to what purpose?

A tap at the door brought Sara round with a start, but it was only Janet come to tell her mistress that dinner was served.

'Yon young devil's gone out then, has he?' she demanded, her sharp beady eyes searching the room. 'Rob thought he heard the car five minutes since.'

'Yes.' Harriet finished her second Scotch and soda and returned her glass to the tray. 'There'll be just the two of us, Janet, so please, let's hear no more about it.'

Dinner was served in an attractively furnished room, with half panelled walls and a beamed ceiling. The rectangular table and heavy chairs matched their surroundings, as did the long serving cabinets and gleaming candelabra.

During the meal, Sara made a conscious effort not to think about Jude, or of his relationship with the woman she had always regarded as her aunt. After all, her position had not significantly changed. She had come here to be Harriet's companion, and the fact that there was someone else living in the house should make no difference. She sighed, as she helped herself to spiced chicken, creamy in its rich white sauce. Why should she feel so surprised anyway? Harriet was still a very attractive woman. It was natural that she should enjoy a man's company. But what really disturbed Sara, if she was totally honest, was the identity of the man involved, and the fact that he must be at least fifteen years younger than Harriet.

When dinner was over, they adjourned to the sitting room where they had had tea. The tray containing the coffee was set between them, and Sara relaxed before the comfortable warmth of the fire. It was going to be all right, she told herself firmly, and ignored the little voice that mocked her inexperience.

While they were eating, Harriet had said little of consequence, the comings and goings of Janet, and the young village girl, who Harriet explained came up daily to help her, serving to make any private conversation impossible. But now that they were alone again Harriet became more loquacious, casting any trace of melancholy aside, and applying herself to learning more about Sara herself.

'Tell me,' she said, confidingly, leaning towards her, 'you're what? Twenty-one years old now?'

'Almost,' Sara agreed, and Harriet continued: 'Twenty, then. Reasonably mature, in these permissive days. You must have had lots of boy-friends, mixing with the kind of people your father generally cultivated.'

Sara shrugged. 'Not many. Daddy—Daddy was quite strict, actually. He—he didn't encourage me to accept invitations from other journalists.'

Harriet seemed pleased. 'No?' She hesitated. 'I suspected as much. Charles, in common with others of his kind, probably followed the maxim, do as I say, not as I do!'

'Daddy wanted to protect me.' Sara could not let Harriet cast any slur on her father's reputation, no matter how deserved. 'But it wasn't necessary,' she added, pleating the skirt of her dress with sudden concentration. 'I was quite capable of taking care of myself. Boarding school taught me a lot.'

Harriet nodded. 'So—no boy-friends?'

Sara shrugged. 'Some.'

'But no one serious.'

'No.' Sara didn't quite know whether she liked this form of questioning, but then she consoled herself with the thought that no doubt Harriet wanted to assure herself that no young man was likely to come and take her away, just as they were getting used to one another.

'Good.' Harriet smiled now. 'I think we're going to get on very well.'

'I hope so.'

Harriet finished her coffee, and then lay back in her chair, regarding Sara with apparent affection. 'You know,' she said, 'I've always wanted a daughter. Someone to talk to, to share my thoughts with, someone young and beautiful like you . . .'

'You're very kind.'

Sara grimaced, but Harriet was serious. 'I mean it,' she said. 'Once I hoped, but—it was not to be.' She shook her head. 'You don't know what it means to me, now that you're here.'

'I just hope I can make myself useful.' Sara paused. 'You still haven't told me what you would like me to do.'

'Oh, don't worry about it.' Harriet lifted her hand, as if it was of no consequence. 'There's plenty of time for that. Settle down first, get the feel of the place, adjust to our way of life. Then we'll start worrying about what there is for you to do.'

Sara sighed. 'I don't want to be a parasite.'

'You won't be that, my dear.'

'No, but—well, if there's not a lot for me to do here, perhaps I could take a job, even a part-time one, to help support——'

'I wouldn't hear of it.' Harriet sat upright. 'I'm not a poor woman, Sara. One extra mouth to feed is not going to bankrupt me. And besides, there'll be plenty for you to do, you'll see.'

Sara was doubtful. Her foolish ideas of changing library books, reading to her aunt, or taking her for drives in the country, seemed so remote now and she didn't honestly see what she could do to earn her keep.

'Now, you'll need some money,' Harriet went on in a

businesslike tone. 'I propose to make you a monthly
allowance, paid in advance, of course, and deposited to
your account at the bank in Buford.'

'I do have a little money,' Sara protested, but Harriet
waved her objections aside.

'Keep it,' she said. 'You don't know when a little capital
might come in handy. Take the allowance, Sara. It would
please me.'

Sara shook her head a trifle bemusedly. She was grateful
to Harriet, more grateful than she could ever say; but
vaguely apprehensive too, although of what she could not
imagine. It was like a dream come true, this house, her
room—Harriet's kindness. Surely even Laura could have
no complaints in such idyllic surroundings.

Jude had not returned when Sara went to bed. Janet
brought hot chocolate and biscuits at ten o'clock, and by
the time Sara had drunk hers, her eyes were drooping. It
had been a long day, and in many ways an exhausting
one, not least on her nerves, and she was relieved when
Harriet suggested she should retire.

'You must get your beauty sleep, darling,' she
remarked, lifting her cheek for Sara to kiss, and the girl
hid her slight embarrassment as she quickly left the room.

The stairs were shadowy, now that the chandelier was
no longer lit, but her room was warm and cosy. Someone
had been in, in her absence, and turned down her bed,
the rose-pink sheets soft and inviting, folded over the
downy quilt.

Sara quickly shed her clothes and replaced them with a
pair of cotton pyjamas. Then, after cleaning her teeth
and removing her make-up, she slid between the sheets
with eager anticipation. It was so good to feel the mattress
yielding to her supple young body, and she curled her
toes deliciously against the silky poplin. Sleep, she
thought, that was what she needed. Right now, her mind
was too confused to absorb any deeper impressions.

She must have fallen asleep immediately. She scarcely

remembered turning out the lamp, but she awakened with a start to find her room in total darkness, so she must have done. She knew at once what had awakened her. The sound was still going on. And she lay there shivering unpleasantly, as the voices that had disturbed her sleep continued. She couldn't hear everything that they were saying. Only now and then, Harriet's voice rose to a crescendo and a tearful phrase emerged above the rest. For the most part it was a low and angry exchange, with Jude's attractive tenor deepened to a harsh and scathing invective.

Sara located the sound as coming from a room some distance along the corridor. Harriet's room perhaps, at its position above the stairs: a likely explanation why their voices carried so well. The echoing vault of the hall would act as an acoustic, throwing the sounds back at her with unwelcome resonance.

Drawing the quilt over her head, she endeavoured to deafen herself to the exchange, but it was impossible. Phrases like: *You don't care how you hurt me*! and *Jude, please*! were unmistakable, and Sara would have rather slept in the stables than be an unwilling witness to such humiliation.

The sounds ceased with sudden abruptness. A door slammed, footsteps sounded—descending the stairs?—and then silence enveloped the old house once again. Sara expelled her breath on a gulp, and only as she did so did she realise she had been holding it. It was stupid, but even her breathing had thundered in her ears while they were rowing, her heart hammering noisily as she struggled to bury her head in the pillows.

Turning on to her back, she now strained her ears to hear anything at all, but there was nothing. Only the haunting cry of an owl as it swooped low over the house disturbed the stillness, and her limbs trembled weakly as she realised it was over.

What time was it? she wondered, and gathering herself

with difficulty, she leaned over and switched on the bed-side lamp. The little carriage clock glinted in the shadows, its pointers showing a quarter to two. Goodness, she thought, switching the light out again, it was the middle of the night!

Of course, it was impossible to get back to sleep again. The first exhausted hours were over, and had she not had the proof of seeing the time for herself, she would have guessed it was almost morning. She felt wide awake, and restless, and with what had just happened to disturb her thoughts she knew it was hopeless to expect to relax.

After lying for perhaps fifteen minutes, staring into the darkness, she leaned over again and switched the lamp back on. The clock chimed as she did so, just one delight-ful little ring to mark the hour, and she gazed at it dis-consolately, wishing it was later. It wouldn't be light for hours and she had learned to hate the darkness since her father's death. She remembered everything connected with *that* night so clearly, not least the clammy coldness of her father's skin when she had tried to wake him . . .

Unable to bear the connotation, Sara swung her legs out of bed and pushed her toes into her slippers. She needed something to make her sleep, but the tablets the doctor had given her she had flushed down the lavatory. And in any case, lately, she had not needed anything. Living with Laura had helped her get things into per-spective, and time and healthy exhaustion had done the rest. But tonight was different. She was in a strange house, in a strange bed—and the argument that had woken her had implications she could not ignore. Was this what her father had meant when he had spoken of Harriet having troubles of her own? Had he known of Jude's existence? Or the relationship between them?

Pulling on a cotton wrapper over her pyjamas, Sara opened her door and listened. The corridor was silent, the only light coming through the window at the end, a silvery moonlight, that turned everything grey.

Sara's tongue circled her lips. Jude had evidently gone to his room. The house was quiet now, and no one would know if she slipped down to the library and helped herself to a drink. Alcohol was the only thing she could think of that might make her drowsy, and she might even take a book from the shelves while she was there, just to help it along.

Drawing her door almost closed, she padded along the corridor and reached the head of the stairs without incident. The hall below was dark and empty, and without giving herself time to speculate upon the possible ghosts which might haunt an old building like this, she ran lightfooted down the stairs.

She was breathing quickly when she reached the hall, but the library door was unmistakable. She remembered exactly where she had been standing when Jude spoke to her earlier, and she crossed to it quickly and turned the handle.

The fire was just a few glowing embers now, enough to give a little warmth but no illumination. With careful precision Sara closed the door behind her, before reaching blindly for the switch.

She felt, rather than heard, the movement behind her, the sudden awareness that she was not alone in the room, that prickled up her spine with icy fingers. Cold panic reigned for only a moment before her hand found the switch, but the frantic flicking of the catch produced no cheering illumination. Either the bulb was defunct or it had been removed—both possibilities offering little in the way of reassurance—and Sara's hand went automatically for the door knob, in a terrified attempt to get out of the room again.

But the door wouldn't open. No matter how she twisted and tugged at the handle, something seemed to be preventing the door from moving, and a sob of hysteria rose in her throat as something brushed over her shoulder.

The flooding warmth of mellow light caused a choking

cry to escape her, followed almost immediately by a sense of bitter resentment. The reason why the door would not open was plain. Jude was leaning against it, his broad shoulders encased only in the brown silk shirt he had been wearing earlier, resting easily against the panels. The thing that had brushed her shoulder must have been his hand, on its way to the switch, although how he had been able to work it when she could not, she couldn't imagine.

But her own anger at his cruel game was more than equalled by the fury in Jude's face, the curiously light eyes gleaming with pure malice as they rested on Sara's flushed cheeks.

'What the hell are you doing down here?' he snapped, before she could gather herself sufficiently to offer her own protest. 'Sneaking about in the dark! What did you expect to find?'

Sara swallowed her indignation. 'I came to get a drink, actually,' she declared, pulling the lapels of her wrapper closer across her throat. 'I had no idea you were in here, or I shouldn't have intruded. And—and in any case, you had no reason to frighten me like that!'

'Frighten you!' Jude's mouth twisted. 'You gave me one hell of a start, creeping in here like some pale wraith at the dead of night!'

'I was not creeping!' Sara resented his tone. 'I—I just didn't want to disturb anyone, that's all.'

Jude straightened away from the door. 'Having been disturbed yourself, one supposes,' he remarked sardonically.

'Well—perhaps.' Sara was loath to admit as much. 'I—I was thirsty, that's all.'

'So you came for—what? Scotch? Sherry? Isn't the water in your bathroom good enough?'

Sara sighed. 'All right. I wanted something to help me get to sleep.'

Jude surveyed her broodingly, one hand searching

inside the unbuttoned front of his shirt. It was a disturbingly sensuous gesture, and one that Sara in her heated emotional state was not unaware of, and she had to drag her eyes away from his lean body and the confusing feelings it engendered.

'Help yourself,' he said, after a moment, and although Sara wanted nothing so much as to get away from him, and the disruptive effect he had on her, she forced herself to cross to the cabinet and pick up a bottle of Scotch.

As she fumbled for a glass, she noticed his jacket thrown carelessly over the desk and another bottle standing significantly beside the sofa. Obviously, that was where he had been sitting—or lying?—when she entered the room, but it still didn't explain how he had been able to turn on the light when she hadn't.

The bottle was hard to open, and as if growing impatient with her uselessness, Jude came and took it from her. The stopper unwound easily beneath his strong fingers, and he poured a generous measure into her glass before closing it again.

'I—that's too much——'

The amount he had given her looked equal to two doubles, and Sara was not sure her head could stand it. She didn't want to spend her first day at Knight's Ferry with a hangover, but his expression mirrored his derision.

'Of course,' he said, with mocking politeness, and before she could make any objection he had lifted the glass to his lips and swallowed half at a gulp. 'Better?'

Sara took the tumbler from him half resentfully, and the grey eyes revealed his awareness of her reluctance to drink from the same glass. It was as if he was, in some obscure way, using her to assuage his own frustrations, and she sensed the dangerous precipitation of his mood.

'Well?' he said. 'Aren't you going to drink it?' and she glanced nervously down at the glass in her hand.

'I—I thought I might take it up to bed,' she said, forcing herself to meet his gaze, and the taunting bitterness of his expression made her wish she had never left her room.

'I guess in that outfit, it's the only offer you're likely to get,' he remarked offensively, and Sara's indignation at last spilled from her.

'It's the only offer I'd want from a parasite like you!' she snapped, ignoring the ominous tautening of his face muscles. 'You may believe your position here entitles you to behave without consideration for anyone's feelings but your own, *I don't*! And I should warn you, if you have conceived any notion that I might provide a passing diversion, forget it! I'm not interested.'

'Aren't you?' The words seemed to be torn from him, the usually light eyes smouldering with a dark and angry flame. 'And what if I don't accept that? What if I choose to prove to you that you could be oh, so wrong? What are you going to do about it?'

Sara's face burned. 'I—I think you've had too much to drink, Mr Jude——' she began, only to break off convulsively when his hand closed round her wrist, forcing her to lift the glass she was holding to her lips.

'Go on,' he said harshly. 'Drink it. Put your lips where mine have been. Sicken yourself!'

Sara gulped. 'You're crazy——'

'Am I?' A dark brow quirked. 'Why? For letting you speak to me like that? Believe it, if you were a man, I'd have knocked your teeth down your throat before now!'

Sara quivered. 'If I was a man, I wouldn't have said it.'

'You might,' he retorted grimly. 'It wasn't all to do with sex, was it? I seem to remember you said something about my being a parasite.'

Sara tried to free her wrist, but all she did was spill Scotch on the carpet. 'I want to go to bed——'

'I am not a parasite, Miss Shelley,' he stated harshly. 'I work for my living, believe me. You'll find out.'

Sara did feel sick now. 'Please let me go,' she begged, tugging away from him, but her behaviour only seemed to incense him further. With a savage twist he took her wrist behind her back and brought her up close to him, the glass spinning heedlessly on to the floor as he bent his head to hers.

'There's more than one way to taste my lips,' he declared, and her knees sagged helplessly as his mouth sought hers.

She had to clutch his arm with her free hand to prevent herself from falling, the taut muscles beneath the silk of his sleeve firm and unyielding. She was aware of so many things in those few seconds—the alcohol flavouring his lips, the hardness of his chest against her breasts, the clean male scent of him, that acted like an intoxicant on senses already inflamed by his arrogance. Even the pain in her arm was numbed by the probing caress of his mouth, as the violence of aggression gave way to a sensual invasion.

He released her arm abruptly as his lips left hers to light a burning trail across her cheek to her ear. His tongue stroked the area behind her ear, where a tiny pulse raced madly, and probed the sensitive skin of her nape, in the scented hollow of her neck. Sara could hardly breathe. Her face was pressed suffocatingly against his throat, and weakness overwhelmed her when his fingers strayed familiarly over her waist and hips, before sliding upward to the fullness of her breast. Her muffled protest was barely audible, and even through the double layer of cotton he must have felt her instinctive response. When his thumb rubbed sensuously over the hardening nipple, her traitorous body softened, and she arched herself unguardedly against him.

The muscled hardness of his thighs made her want to part her legs to accommodate him, and she sensed his quickened breathing as his mouth returned to hers. Searching deeply and persuasively, it plundered her trembling lips until she had no will to resist him: and her fingers sought the hair at his nape to hold him even closer. She felt the unfamiliar pressure that swelled against her, the pulsating heat of his manhood as it sought a closer intimacy: but it was his strangled oath that separated them, and the violent thrust of his hands.

'Get out of here!' he muttered, turning abruptly away from her, and Sara swayed confusedly, bemused by his sudden rejection. 'Go back to bed!' he grated, breathing deeply as he spread his palms on the desk, and the whole horror of her submission swept over her.

'Still here?'

The hateful derision in his voice brought her quickly to her senses, particularly as he had evidently recovered his composure, and had straightened away from the desk to regard her sardonically. Sara wrapped her own arms about her body, wishing she knew some way to wipe that scornful expression from his face, and unconsciously chose just the way to do it.

'Thank you,' she said, and his features tightened ominously. 'Thank you for confirming the opinion I'd formed of you. I just wonder what your employer would say if she knew how you'd abused your position!'

CHAPTER FOUR

SAFE in her room again, albeit without the Scotch she had ventured downstairs to get, Sara succumbed to a total sense of lassitude. She felt sick and shaken and weak with revulsion, her whole being shrinking from the scene that had just taken place. Had it really happened? Had she actually incited Jude to physical violence? And was it really such a short step from there to savage violation? She couldn't believe it. She didn't want to believe it. But her arm still ached where he had twisted it, and her legs were not trembling for nothing.

Sinking down on to the side of the bed, she gave way to a

shuddering reaction, pushing her fingers into her hair and turning her head from side to side. How could he? she breathed. How could he have done it? Whatever she had said to taunt him, how could he have treated her that way? She was a relative of his employer, a guest in the house. His behaviour was disgusting, and completely unforgivable.

Yet— Her hands fell to her lap and she gazed at her pale reflection, mirrored in the glass above the dressing table. Had her own behaviour been so blameless? When he caressed her breast, had she thrust him away? When his tongue had stroked her mouth, had she pressed her lips together? And when she felt the shameless length of him thrust against her thighs, had she squeezed her legs together and denied the provocation?

She knew she had not. To her eternal shame, she must accept that somehow he had overcome her natural reticence and invaded that part of her which hitherto she had been able to control. Indeed, until tonight she would never have believed any man could so subjugate her to his will. But now she had learned that this was not so, and she must guard against anything like it ever happening again. It was frightening to suspect that one might not always be in control of one's own destiny, and her hands shook unsteadily as she twisted them together.

Perhaps it was just a passing thing, she thought, seeking to excuse herself. Her father's death had been a terrible shock. She might be more susceptible because of her disturbed emotional condition, although that in itself did not explain her wanton behaviour. What must Jude have thought, when she arched herself against him? she wondered in dismay. What false opinion of her must he have formed because of her abandoned conduct? Perhaps he had assumed she was used to men touching her in that way. Her skin crept at the thought.

With burning cheeks she got up from the bed to remove her wrapper, her reflection drawing her attention once again. Her mouth was soft, bruised, and when she touched it with a trembling finger, she winced as her tongue tasted blood. Dear God, she thought wildly, how on earth was she going to face Harriet in the morning? And what could she say if Jude chose to betray her?

Her parting words to him threatening as much had been simply bravado. How could she tell Harriet what he had done, when by doing so she could only cause her pain? But equally, how could she go on living in the same house as a man who had shown he had no respect for any woman?

To her dismay, Sara was awakened by Harriet herself, with a breakfast tray. Her face hot with embarrassment, she scrambled up on to her pillows as the older woman stood smiling down at her, and realised with anxious misgivings that this was another point against her.

However, Harriet wouldn't listen to any apologies about oversleeping, and seated herself on the end of the bed, evidently prepared to stay and chat. 'I knew you'd be tired, my dear,' she declared, her calm expression showing no signs of the distress she had suffered the night before. 'I said to Janet, we'll let her sleep. After all, there's nothing spoiling.'

'But what time is it?' Sara shifted unhappily, the full recollection of the night's events returning with unpleasant definition. If she had overslept, it was hardly surprising. Her troubled brain had not succumbed to exhaustion before the first birds began their morning chorus.

'It's a little after ten o'clock,' Harriet replied blandly, and Sara almost overset the orange juice on the tray.

'Ten!' she echoed blankly. 'Oh, Harriet! What must you think of me? I can't remember when I last stayed in bed until this time.'

'Then it will do you good,' averred Harriet firmly, pointing to the tray. 'Go ahead, eat your breakfast. We can talk as you enjoy your meal.'

In all honesty, Sara would have been satisfied with orange juice and coffee. Her head felt heavy, and the prospect of the day ahead filled her with apprehension.

But because Harriet was there, watching her, she managed to eat a slice of toast and marmalade as well.

'I thought you'd prefer the more continental style of breakfast to bacon and eggs,' Harriet remarked, as Sara buttered her toast. 'I never touch fried food myself, but Jude generally has the whole bit—cereal, bacon, toast!' She lifted her shoulders in a gesture of distaste. 'Yet he never seems to put on weight as I do.'

It was Sara's opportunity to mention what had happened the night before, but of course she remained silent. She could not bring herself to destroy their association, before it had even begun—and he probably knew that, *damn him*! she thought, clenching her fist—before discovering Harriet was watching her with a curious expression on her face.

'Tell me,' she said, and Sara felt a wave of colour sweep up her throat at the anticipated question, 'you weren't disturbed last night, were you?'

'Disturbed?'

Sara repeated the word to give herself time to think, but Harriet took it as an answer. 'Obviously you weren't,' she said, with evident relief, fingering the double string of pearls that circled her throat. 'Er—there was some disturbance outside. Poachers, I should imagine. Lord Hadley's gamekeepers often come across traps that the village youths set to catch hares and rabbits, and while they're a nuisance —the rabbits, I mean—trespassing is an offence.'

Sara poured herself coffee, steadying the pot with both hands. For an awful moment she had wondered if Jude had divulged her visit to the library the night before, suitably edited, of course, to cast suspicion on her motives. After all, there had been that argument between Jude and her aunt, and she would hate Harriet to think she had been spying on her.

'It's a lovely morning,' Harriet declared now, getting up from the bed and crossing to the windows to draw the flimsy drapes aside. 'See, the sun is shining. I thought we might go for a walk after you're dressed.'

'Oh, yes. Yes, I'd like that.'

Sara thrust the tray aside, determining not to let the night's events spoil her first day at Knight's Ferry, and Harriet came back to the bed to smile affectionately down at her.

'I thought we might walk up to Linden Court,' she said. 'So wear something nice. Lord Hadley has an eye for a pretty girl, and you really are—exceptionally pretty.'

It was a little disconcerting having to choose something suitable to wear, but at least it was distracting. Left to herself, Sara would probably have worn jeans and a chunky sweater, but Harriet's request had left her in something of a quandary. She could wear a skirt, she supposed, but surely trousers were more suitable for walking in the country. And besides, she wasn't at all sure she wanted to catch the eye of some spry old man, whose only claim to fame was an hereditary title.

She eventually compromised, and chose a dark brown corded pants suit, the waist-length jerkin accentuating her slim waist and the swelling contours of her hips. With it she wore a cream knitted cotton shirt, leaving the top two buttons unfastened to expose the plain gold chain which had been her father's last present to her.

Janet appeared to collect her breakfast tray as Sara was putting her bed straight, and the elderly housekeeper looked somewhat taken aback to find the girl doing her job.

'There's no need for you to make your bed, miss,' she declared tersely. 'I can just as easily do it, when I'm doing the others.'

'I don't mind, really.' Sara straightened the quilt and stood up. 'I'm not a guest here, Janet, I'm here to work. And if there's any way I can help you, please just let me know.'

Janet sniffed. 'You're Miss Ferrars' niece, miss. That's family. And family don't make beds. Not while I'm here to do it.'

There was no trace of warmth in her voice as she said this, and Sara gave up. 'Very well. If you don't want me to make the bed, I won't. But I meant what I said. I do want to help.'

'Huh!' Janet snorted, and as Sara was going out of the door, she saw the Scotswoman throw back the quilt and begin tugging the sheet free of the mattress. It was a blatant display of wilfulness, and Sara felt absurdly hurt as she went down the stairs.

She looked about her somewhat apprehensively as she entered Harriet's sitting room, but there was only Harriet in the room, seated at the desk. She looked up with a smile as Sara appeared in the doorway, and the girl stepped eagerly into the room as she put down her pen.

'Very nice,' said Harriet, getting up from her chair, and viewing the girl with critical eyes. 'Are you ready? I was just preparing tonight's menu while I waited. You do like most things, I hope. You're not a finicky eater.'

'Oh, no.' Sara shook her head. 'I don't have many preferences. Living—living with Daddy, I had to get used to all kinds of food.'

'Of course.' Harriet's eyes were sympathetic. 'Well, shall we go? I've told Janet where we'll be.'

Sara nodded, and Harriet picked up a sheepskin jacket as they left the room. This morning the older woman was dressed in tweeds and a silk blouse, but once again her style and elegance would have complimented a woman half her age.

It was crisp outside, still quite chilly, but wonderfully fresh. Sara, remembering London and the pervading smell of diesel in the parks there, breathed deeply, inhaling the fragrance of tulips and irises, growing in abundance along the paths.

To her relief, there was no sign of Jude as they emerged into the spring sunlight. Only an elderly man could be seen, working in the borders of the drive, and he raised his cap to Harriet as she called a greeting, before returning to his labours with evident enjoyment.

'Rob,' said Harriet, by way of an explanation, as they took the path that led around the side of the house. 'Janet's husband. He looks after the gardens, tends to the car, that sort of thing. And he's quite a useful plumber and electrician, if he puts his mind to it.'

Sara nodded. 'A handyman, in fact.'

'Indeed,' Harriet agreed. 'I don't know what I'd do without them.'

'Do they have any children?' asked Sara, following Harriet past a well-tended vegetable garden to where a high brick wall marked the boundary of the stables. They could hear the horses long before they could see them, and Sara's nails curled into her palms in expectation of the coming confrontation.

'Fortunately no,' Harriet was replying, as they entered the stable yard. 'Fortunately for me, I mean. Janet has markedly motherly tendencies. I fear children would have interfered with her dedication to her job.'

Sara thought that she had not noticed such tendencies in Janet, but then she hardly knew the woman. And it had been evident that she had real affection for her employer. Perhaps Harriet was a little selfish in thinking of herself first, though no doubt Janet was quite content in the niche she had contrived for herself.

A boy of perhaps sixteen years was in the process of grooming a tall chestnut stallion when the two women appeared. It was a beautiful animal, its coat sleek and shining, and it tossed its head arrogantly as Harriet approached.

'Now, now, Minstrel,' she soothed the horse gently, and it allowed her to put her palm on its muzzle, and stroke its mettlesome head. 'Isn't he lovely?' she asked of Sara, as the boy stood politely waiting to one side. 'All of five thousand pounds of horseflesh! But don't you think he's worth it?'

Sara had never been close to such equine perfection,

every inch of its coat polished and gleaming. She even forgot her apprehension in her admiration of the beast, and when a man's voice spoke behind them she started in confusion.

Her involuntary movement made the horse prance about a little skittishly, and the boy took possession of the controlling rein, walking the animal about the yard until it was calm.

And it was all for nothing, thought Sara impatiently. The man in a sweater and riding breeches who had heard their voices and come to join them was not Jude, but an older individual, with greying brown hair and a gingery moustache.

'Lovely morning, Miss Ferrars,' he greeted Harriet politely, switching his gaze to Sara and including her in the salutation. 'I see you've been showing this young lady our prize exhibit. But did you know Midnight foaled this morning?'

'No!' Harriet clapped her hands together. 'I—well, I haven't spoken to Jude this morning. I imagine he was here. He hasn't slept in his room for nights.'

The man nodded. 'He was here, Miss Ferrars. Gave her support, that he did. Come and see the result. I think you'll be pleased.'

The stable was dark after the brightness outside, and warmly redolent of leather and disinfectant. The man led the way to the stall farthest from the entrance, and Sara leaned over a half door to see a wobbly-legged colt nuzzling its mother's thighs. To her immense relief they were alone, and she could only assume that Jude was in bed, sleeping off the effects of his broken night.

'Isn't he beautiful?' Harriet broke into excited laughter. 'Oh, Barnes, do you think he might emulate his father? Just imagine—a two-year-old to equal Mazarin!'

The groom chuckled. 'You're going some, Miss Ferrars. That little stud hasn't even had his first feed yet. You leave him to me. We'll make another Minstrel of him yet.'

Harriet sighed, and Sara followed her rather reluctantly out of the stables. The little creature had been fascinating, but listening to Harriet and the man, Barnes, talking, it appeared the older woman's interest in horses stemmed only from a desire to breed a winner. Sara was disappointed. She liked animals, and in spite of what she had said to Jude, she had looked forward to riding again. But judging by the thoroughbreds she had seen, there was nothing here suitable to her limited talents.

Leaving the stables behind, they struck out across open parkland towards the grey walls of Linden Court. Set on its knoll, with the sunlight reflecting from its many window panes, it looked tall and majestic, and Sara couldn't help a certain thrill of anticipation at the prospect of meeting its owner. It seemed so unlikely that anyone could own anything so huge and stately, and she wondered again at Harriet's connections with the family. She supposed it accounted for the fact that Jude called Lord Hadley's son by his given name, although in that regard, Rupert Hadley had not behaved with any distinction. Indeed, if she had not known better, she would have supposed their positions were reversed, with Jude displaying all the arrogance one might expect from landed aristocracy.

There were deer in the park, shy creatures that quivered in the shade of budding chestnut trees, watching their progress with wide nervous eyes. Below the terrace of the house, carefully tended lawns disclosed croquet hoops, and away to the right were the netted walls of tennis courts.

'The grounds are open to the public on certain days of the week, all the year round,' Harriet offered, as Sara gazed about her. 'And part of the house is open, too, from May until October. Not the family apartments, of course.'

Sara nodded, and checked her boots for mud as they climbed the steps to the terrace that ran along this side of the building. A peacock strutted proudly away as they crossed the flagged walk, uttering its own peculiar cry as it disappeared among the rhododendrons.

'Who lives here now?' Sara asked, as they approached an arched door, set at one end of the terrace. Evidently this was not the front of the house, but Harriet seemed to know where she was going.

Harriet paused to speak to her. 'Don't look so apprehensive, darling. There's only James and Rupert. Oh, and Venetia, of course. But she doesn't really count.'

Sara frowned. 'Who is Venetia?' She shrugged a little blankly. 'Who is James?'

'James? Why, James Hadley, of course. Rupert's father.'

'Sara gulped. 'You mean—*Lord* Hadley?'

'Who else?' Harriet shrugged. 'Oh, isn't this nice! Our host has come to meet us.'

Sara turned as a man of about sixty emerged from the building. Tall, and still very erect, he crossed the terrace towards them with an easy, loose-limbed stride that denied the lines that bracketed his face, and the iron grey hair lifting in the breeze. He was wearing brown trousers and a tweed jacket, and his clean-shaven face was friendly as he took hold of Harriet's hand.

'I saw you from the window,' he declared, and Harriet smiled in return.

'How nice of you to come and meet us,' she declared. 'James, this is Sara. Quite a surprise, isn't she?'

'How could any relative of yours surprise me?' remarked Lord Hadley gallantly, shaking the girl's hand. 'How do you do, Sara. Welcome to Linden Court.'

'Thank you.' Sara found herself smiling too. He was so unexpectedly nice, and approachable, and she saw Harriet nodding approvingly as their host ushered them into the house.

They entered the private wing of the building, the square carpeted hallway giving access to the family apartments, Lord Hadley explained, for Sara's benefit. It was not unlike Knight's Ferry, with its panelled walls

and curved ceiling, but the coat of arms above the fireplace was rather feudal, and it was on a much larger scale.
Two dogs rose from their position in front of the fire that
burned in the immense hearth as they entered the hall.
Irish wolfhounds, Sara guessed, admiring their proud
shaggy heads, and their host involuntarily confirmed this
opinion as he drew her attention to them.

'Did you ever see two such hapless creatures?' he
declared, as they came to examine the new arrivals. 'My
son bought them as watchdogs, but as you can see, they're
not much use. If you don't cause a fuss, they'll eat out of
your hand.'

'They are beautiful, though,' Sara exclaimed, as one of
them licked her fingers. 'What are their names?'

'Troilus and Cressida,' he responded wryly. 'My son's
choice, of course. We call them Troy and Cress for short.'
He shook his head. 'Come along. We'll have coffee in the
morning room.'

The morning room turned out to be a comfortable
living room, its plain walls adorned with hunting prints.
A wide fireplace smouldered with logs, and two huge sofas
faced one another across an Oriental rug. The walls were
lined with cabinets containing a variety of glass and china
ware, and two round tables stood in the window embras-
ures, spread with copies of *Horse and Hound* and *Country
Life*.

Lord Hadley saw his guests seated and then rang the
bell for service. As he stood between them on the hearth,
Sara couldn't help thinking how typical of the country
gentleman he was, the stem of a pipe visible above the
pocket on his breast, his booted feet set apart, the leather
highly polished.

A young maid appeared and coffee was ordered, and
then Harriet asked where Rupert was. 'Oh, I expect he's
about somewhere,' replied Lord Hadley carelessly. 'He
almost had an accident yesterday, riding in the lane. I
shouldn't have known about it, I suppose, but Juniper

pulled a tendon getting out of the path of a car, and that had to be explained. Silly young blighter! The sooner he's married and learns some responsibility the better.'

'Yes.' Harriet relaxed against the cushioned upholstery, her eyes flickering thoughtfully over Sara as she crossed her shapely legs. Then, before the girl could begin to feel uncomfortable, her attention shifted to their host again, and she gave him her most charming smile. 'Jude did say something about it,' she ventured casually. 'Rupert really should learn not to use the public highway as a point-to-point course.'

'Jude?' Lord Hadley returned her look with beetling brows. 'What does Jude know about it? He didn't mention anything to me.'

While Sara was digesting this startling statement, Harriet spoke again with drawling inconsequence. 'Didn't he tell you, James? It was his car Rupert almost jumped into. Jude was on his way back from collecting Sara at the station. As you can imagine, he got quite a shock.'

Lord Hadley smothered an oath as the maid tapped at the door. He waited with evident impatience while she came in and put down the tray, and set out the coffee cups and saucers. Then, informing her shortly that they could serve themselves, he sent her about her business, before seating himself grimly beside Harriet on the sofa.

Sara, watching this display, was slightly puzzled by Harriet's involvement of Jude. For some reason, the younger man had seen Lord Hadley since yesterday, and evidently he had said nothing about what had happened. What point was there in labouring the incident, for no apparent reason than to cause trouble for Rupert?

'Are you telling me Rupert jumped the fence?' James Hadley demanded now, and Harriet made a token effort to retrieve herself.

'I've probably spoken out of turn,' she exclaimed, but Sara found she couldn't quite believe this statement. 'I was sure Rupert would have told you. Jude introduced him to Sara.'

'Did he?' Lord Hadley's gaze rested briefly on the girl's faintly embarrassed features. 'No. He said nothing to me. I shall have a few words with him, when the opportunity arises.'

'Oh, dear, have I said the wrong thing?' Harriet was almost convincing in her distress. 'James, please don't tell Jude that I've told you. I naturally assumed that you knew.'

'Mmm.'

Lord Hadley did not sound as if he entirely believed her, but good manners forbore a plainer comment. Instead, it was left to Harriet to offer to pour the coffee, and afterwards, to ask warmly about Venetia.

Sara, listening to her aunt enquiring about this unknown female, wondered at her capacity for deception. Only minutes before, she had dismissed Sara's own question about her as of no account, but now it transpired that she was Lord Hadley's daughter.

'Such a sweet child,' declared Harriet gently. 'I'm sure Sara would love to meet her. She needs some friends of her own age in the vicinity, and I'm sure Venetia would welcome a companion.'

'You may be right.' Lord Hadley was polite, but Sara thought it was becoming increasingly obvious that he was not enthusiastic about her becoming friendly with either of his offspring. Perhaps it was a false impression, but she had the feeling that Harriet knew exactly how he felt, and for reasons of her own she was determined to thwart him.

The coffee was hot and strong, and to Sara's relief the subject of the near-accident was not mentioned again. Instead, her host asked her about India, where he had been stationed during the last war, and offered his condolences about her father, without being overly sympathetic.

It was as they were rising to take their leave that they

heard voices in the hall outside. Harriet appeared to have abandoned her attempts to bring her niece and the younger Hadleys together for today, but as they turned towards the door it opened to admit two people. One was a girl of perhaps Sara's age, smaller and darker, and infinitely sturdier. The other was Jude.

Sara fell back a step, her eyes going automatically to Harriet before returning to the newcomers. What on earth was Jude doing here? she wondered in dismay. Unless this was the girl with whom he had spent the previous evening. Her mouth felt dry, and she didn't know where to look. Particularly as the other girl was looking at her in a far from friendly fashion.

Jude, it had to be said, did not look at all perturbed. And there was no evidence in his lean sardonic face that he had spent a disturbed night. On the contrary, he looked just as relaxed and confident as ever, and when his silver-grey eyes met hers, there was no trace of familiarity in their depths. On the contrary, they were the eyes of a stranger, and Sara wondered rather wildly whether she had imagined that scene taking place in the library.

The girl went straight to Lord Hadley, reaching up to kiss his cheek. 'Hello, Daddy,' she said, establishing their relationship. 'I hope you don't mind. I've persuaded Jude to take me into Buford.'

'Have you?' Lord Hadley's eyes met Jude's above her head, and Sara saw the interrogation of that exchange.

'I did finish those letters before I committed myself,' the younger man offered, in way of mitigation, and Sara blinked in confusion as Lord Hadley shook his head.

'Jude isn't here to entertain you, Venetia,' he declared, looking down at his daughter. 'He works for me, you know, and I'd prefer it if you asked me before bothering him.'

While Sara absorbed this amazing revelation, Venetia's full mouth jutted sulkily. 'But, Daddy, I want Jude to take me. I like going with him. Don't be a meanie! You know I can't drive myself.'

Lord Hadley glanced rather meaningfully at Harriet, and she moved her shoulders in a faintly derogatory gesture. 'You know how it is to be young,' she murmured, much to Sara's astonishment. 'I'm sure Jude's not neglecting his work, James. Why not let them go? You can't keep them always on a chain.'

'That's right, Daddy.' Venetia cast a grateful glance in Harriet's direction. 'Why shouldn't I have some fun? Besides, Jude promised——'

'Venetia, I do not enjoy arguing with you in front of our guests,' her father replied brusquely. 'Nor do I keep you on a chain. Jude's simply too polite to tell you you're wasting his time.'

Venetia gasped and turned indignantly to the younger man. 'That's not true, is it, Jude? I'm not a nuisance, am I?'

'I'm sure you're not.' Once again, Harriet intervened, approaching Lord Hadley with wide disarming eyes. 'James, don't be a spoilsport. Why shouldn't they spend a couple of hours in Buford? What harm can it do?'

James Hadley looked as if he would like to have said something further, but his innate good manners prevented him. Instead he turned to Jude, and the younger man moved his shoulders indifferently.

'As Sara can drive, why don't you ask her to take Venetia to Buford?' he suggested, evoking a speculative stare from Harriet, and Sara felt totally confused. She didn't understand any of this—not Harriet's approval of Jude's friendship with Venetia, surely a dangerous temptation for a man like him, nor Jude's apparent unwillingness to take advantage of this situation. It didn't make sense, unless he was trying to prove his devotion to the older woman, and if so, why was Harriet having to consider his proposition?

She was brought back to the present with a start to find everyone looking at her with varying degrees of anticipation. 'I—I beg your pardon,' she said, realising something must have been asked of her while she was lost in thought, and Lord Hadley drew an impatient breath.

'My father was asking whether you had any objections to driving me to Buford,' Venetia declared, her face taut with resentment. 'Don't put yourself out on my account. Barnes can take me equally as well.'

'Temper, temper, Vennie,' Jude remarked behind her, and Sara shook her head helplessly.

'I—Harriet——' she began awkwardly, but the older woman only shrugged her shoulders.

'If you would like to go with Venetia, don't worry about me,' she declared, apparently approving of Jude's suggestion. 'Have lunch together.' She paused. 'As I said earlier, you should have friends of your own age.'

Her gaze lingered deliberately on Lord Hadley as she said this, and Sara couldn't make up her mind whether he was aware of Harriet achieving her objective. Perhaps he saw her as the lesser of two evils, she thought flatly, wishing she understood what was going on. But Jude's face was enigmatic, and Lord Hadley was looking at the younger man with a curiously rueful expression. Only Venetia's feelings were open and unconcealed, and Sara was left in little doubt as to her opinion of the proposed arrangements.

'If—if Miss Hadley——'

'*Lady* Venetia,' inserted the girl, rather rudely, and Sara revised her estimation of the other girl's character. She was evidently spoilt as well as wilful, and Sara's sympathies hardened.

'Very well, Lady Venetia,' she agreed smoothly, before anyone else could intervene, 'I suggest you make other arrangements.'

Just for an instant she thought Jude's face mirrored mild approval, but then Lord Hadley stepped between them. 'Come, come, Venetia,' he said, and Sara could tell he was annoyed by his daughter's behaviour. 'We'll have no more of this. If Sara is willing to take you, I suggest you accept her offer. Well?'

In her position, Sara felt sure she would have abandoned the whole idea, but Venetia was already faltering. 'I asked Jude,' she protested weakly. 'But—oh, very well, if you insist.'

'Good. Good.' Lord Hadley patted her shoulder approvingly, and then turned to Sara in faint apology.

'You will forgive Venetia, won't you, my dear?' he asserted, and catching Harriet's warning eye, Sara gave in.

'If—Lady Venetia is sure——' The name stuck in her throat but what choice did she have? With Jude and her aunt watching her predicament with equally guarded expressions, she felt ridiculously as if she was being manipulated. And she could do nothing about it.

CHAPTER FIVE

THEIR transport turned out to be a sleek red Porsche, and as Sara fitted herself behind the wheel, she wondered that Venetia could let anyone else drive it. She knew if she owned such a vehicle, no one else would chauffeur her, but perhaps Venetia felt differently. Besides, she had said she *couldn't* drive herself, and it was nothing to do with Sara anyway.

Lord Hadley had given her directions, even though Venetia obviously knew the way, and he and Harriet came out to see them off. Sara waited patiently while Venetia fastened her safety belt, but she couldn't deny the thrill of excitement that gripped her when she at last released the clutch and the powerful car surged forward.

The gravelled drive gave on to a private road that ran through the park, with cattle grids guarding the separate grazing areas. But when they came to the gates that opened on to the highway, Venetia remained in her seat and let Sara climb out to open them, and later to close the same. Re-settling herself in the driving seat, Sara refused to let the other girl's manner upset her, and as the Porsche gathered speed, she gave herself up to the pure delight of unrestricted power. She had driven many vehicles in her short life, from her father's ancient Volvo to an equally ancient Land Rover, in the hills above Jaipur. But she had never had control of a car like this, and her enjoyment seemed to communicate itself to the other girl.

'You drive well,' Venetia remarked grudgingly, after they had been travelling for several minutes. 'I thought you'd be a drag, but you do have a certain flair for it.'

'Well, thank you.' Sara took her eyes from the road for just a second to acknowledge the reluctant tribute. 'Don't you drive?'

Venetia expelled her breath indifferently. 'I used to. And I will again, once I get my licence back.'

Sara's lips parted. 'You're—barred?'

'Isn't it obvious?' Venetia sniffed. 'Oh, I knocked a boy off a moped, six months ago. They said I was driving dangerously. What they omitted to say was that he was a halfwit to be on the road without a crash helmet.'

'I see.' Sara was beginning to understand. 'And the boy—was he hurt?'

Venetia turned to stare out of the window. 'Not seriously. A few broken bones, that's all. He should have seen me coming.'

'Yes.' Sara's response was guarded. She didn't want to disagree with her, but it sounded as if Venetia had been as reckless as her brother with his horse.

'I suppose you think I deserve it,' Venetia added, turning to look at her companion. 'You don't like me much, do you? Admit it. I don't blame you. I don't much like you either.'

Sara shook her head. 'I don't know you well enough to judge,' she exclaimed, half amused by the other girl's candour. 'But I have to say I didn't ask to play chauffeur. Your father fixed it up.'

'Oh, I know.' Venetia plucked at her pleated kilt. The outfit she was wearing did not compliment her plumpness, and Sara wondered whether her father chose her clothes as well. 'It's all Jude's fault really. If he'd really wanted to go, Daddy wouldn't have stopped him.'

Sara absorbed this in silence, and Venetia gave another heartfelt sigh. 'He really is a bastard! There are times when I wish I didn't care what he did, but I *do*!'

Sara slowed to run through a village, glad of the attention needed to negotiate a row of parked cars to avoid making any direct response, and Venetia glanced at her impatiently.

'What do you think of him? Jude, I mean. I suppose you knew him before you came yesterday.'

'No.' Sara braked hard as a little girl skipped into the road in front of the car. She tried to be casual. 'I haven't seen Harriet for years, and then only when she visited me at school.'

'Oh, I see.' Venetia grimaced. 'I don't suppose he'd want to go along on those kind of outings. I, of course, have known him for years, ever since I was a little girl.' She hunched her shoulders. 'That's the trouble.'

'Trouble?' Sara picked up the word, and Venetia nodded.

'I'm crazy about him,' she declared emotively. 'Isn't it painfully obvious?'

Sara didn't know how to reply. Venetia's words had robbed her of breath. It was the last thing she had expected, and yet, now she came to think of it, she had been incredibly slow to understand the real reasons for Venetia's antipathy.

'Well?' The girl was waiting for a reply, and Sara's tongue circled her dry lips. 'I know Harriet doesn't approve,' Venetia went on. 'Oh, she appeared to take my side just now, but that was only to thwart Daddy. She knew if she pushed him far enough, he'd be forced to make a stand.'

Sara shook her head. 'You mean your father doesn't approve of Jude?' she ventured, forced to make some comment, and Venetia grimaced.

'He wants me to marry someone with lots of money *and* a title,' she exclaimed bitterly. 'He won't listen to what *I* want!'

Sara's fingers tightened on the wheel. 'I'm sure your father knows best,' she observed, feeling incapable of making any objective comment, and Venetia snorted.

'I suppose I should have expected that,' she muttered. 'I saw the way you were looking at him. You find him attractive, too, don't you?' She gave a careless shrug of her shoulders. 'That's why we aren't likely to be friends. I don't like competition.'

Sara gasped. 'I—you're wrong——'

'What? About you liking Jude?' Venetia's lips twisted. 'I don't think so.'

'I—I find him arrogant and insolent!' Sara declared hotly. 'I don't know how Harriet——' She broke off abruptly, realising what she had been about to say, and revised it to: 'I don't know how she puts up with him living in her house.'

Venetia regarded her consideringly. 'You know, I almost believe you.'

'You can please yourself.' Sara was indignant. 'I don't tell lies, *Lady* Venetia!'

'Oh, you can skip the formality,' Venetia remarked off-handedly. 'I was just being bitchy earlier. Now you know why.'

Sara caught her lower lip between her teeth. Then, taking a deep breath, she said: 'What I can't understand is, if your father is so opposed to you associating with—with Jude, why does he allow him in the house?'

'Oh, that.' Venetia hunched her shoulders. 'Jude's worked for Daddy for years. Ever since he got his degree. Long before I became a problem.'

'I see.' Sara thought she was beginning to understand. It must have been through Harriet's friendship with Lord Hadley that she had first met Jude. The reasons for his living at Knight's Ferry were less obvious, but no doubt all would be revealed in time. It explained a lot, not least Jude's familiarity with Rupert.

'So that's enough about me,' Venetia remarked now, moving so that she could look at Sara without turning her head. 'Tell me about you. Daddy said something about your father dying rather suddenly, and Harriet offering you a home.'

'Yes, that's right.' Sara didn't mind talking about herself. It was safer. 'My father died nearly three months ago, and Harriet very kindly asked me if I'd like to come and work for her.'

'Work for her?' Venetia's brow furrowed. 'As what?'

'Oh—I don't know exactly. Secretary, perhaps. Companion. I'm afraid my duties aren't awfully clear yet. I think Harriet wants me to settle down first.'

'Mmm.' Venetia was thoughtful. 'Not very exciting, is it?'

'I don't want excitement,' declared Sara flatly. 'I had enough excitement with my father.'

'Oh? Why?'

Sara sighed. 'He was a foreign correspondent and he took me with him on his assignments. We went all over the world.' She paused. 'We never had a permanent home, just a lot of rented houses and hotel rooms.'

'How marvellous!' Venetia was impressed. 'I should love that.'

'Would you?' Sara was sceptical. 'Well, it's over now, and—and I'm not sorry.'

'You're not sorry your father's dead?' exclaimed Venetia, shocked, and Sara resignedly inclined her head.

'Oh yes, I'm sorry he's dead. But I never want to live like that again. It's too—uncertain.'

'You sound bitter.'

'Do I?' Sara expelled her breath reflectively. 'I was, but not any more.'

Venetia looked puzzled, but she didn't labour the point, and Sara was relieved. Curiously enough, it was true. The bitterness she had nurtured since her father's suicide was fading, and she hoped that in time she would be able to face the memory of what had happened without resentment.

Buford was a small market town set about a central square, which had now been designated a shopping precinct. There were plenty of modern stores, side by side with the more traditional shops, and several attractively preserved Tudor houses, converted to museums.

On Venetia's instructions Sara parked the Porsche in the newly-constructed multi-storey car-park, and then the two girls strolled around the square. Sara relaxed as the conversation turned to clothes and fashion, and she was able to give the other girl her opinion of the kind of things she thought would suit her.

'I get most of my clothes in London, of course,' Venetia remarked with unconscious hauteur, but Sara casually pointed out that expensive clothes were not always the most attractive.

'I think you would suit something like that,' she suggested, indicating a slim-fitting tailored skirt and jacket on a model in the window of a popular chain store, and Venetia's nose wrinkled.

'Do you think so?' she asked doubtfully. 'It's awfully plain.'

'I think plain garments are flattering, providing you can wear them,' replied Sara innocently. 'With your hair being shoulder-length and curly, you can afford to wear something less fussy.'

'Do you mean it?' Venetia was evidently interested.

'Oh, but you wear plain things, and your hair is straight.'
She grimaced. 'I think what you mean is, I would look
slimmer in a straight skirt.'

'And don't you want to do that?' Sara didn't try to lie
to her, and Venetia turned away.

'Perhaps. I don't think it's anything to do with you.'

'I'm sorry.' Sara pushed her hands into the pockets of
her jerkin. 'Shall we go?'

'Yes.'

Venetia squared her shoulders and walked on, but Sara
noticed she did cast a thoughtful look over her shoulder,
as if she hadn't been entirely unconvinced.

They had lunch in a hotel, an oak-beamed establish-
ment, where Venetia was instantly recognisable, and
therefore instantly served. They ate pâté and fried chick-
en, and finished with a strawberry gâteau that Sara
would never have chosen for herself. But Venetia ate
everything that was put before her, and the reasons for her
being overweight were not hard to find.

Afterwards she spent some time at the cosmetic counter
of the biggest store in Buford, before walking back to the
car. She spent well over twenty pounds on various creams
and lotions, but Sara made no further comment about
her appearance. She had no desire to promote another
argument, and besides, she had other things to think
about.

As she drove back to King's Priory, the memory of the
previous night's events returned like a nagging thorn in
her side. Now that she knew Jude worked for Lord
Hadley, she had to admit he had had reason to be angry.
It didn't excuse the way he had behaved, that was unforgivable, but she felt ashamed of having called him a
parasite when that was patently not true.

Venetia didn't talk much on the homeward journey
either. She was quite content examining the jars and tubes
of perfumed ointment she had bought, and Sara concen-
trated on the traffic, wondering if she would ever be

invited to drive the car again.

It was almost four o'clock when they got back to Linden Court, and as Sara parked the car in the drive, a young man emerged from the house. It was Rupert. She recognised him instantly, even though he looked somewhat different in well-cut slacks and a silk shirt, a floral cravat filling the opened neck. However, although his expression was far from contented, his deferential manner was unmistakeable.

'Hello, Miss Shelley,' he greeted Sara politely, as both girls got out of the car. 'Hello there, Vennie. Had a good shopping spree? I see Marshalls will need to replenish their stocks.'

'Don't be an ass, Rupert.' Venetia spoke without malice. 'I've hardly bought anything at all.' She studied him perceptively, and then glanced at Sara. 'What's up? Is it something I said?'

'Jude blew the gaff about me riding in the lane!' her brother declared resentfully, pushing his hands into his pockets. Then giving Sara an apologetic look, he muttered: 'I know it was bloody silly, but I never thought Jude was a sneak!'

'He didn't——'

The words were out before Sara could prevent them. After her own guilty feelings on the way home, she could not prevent the instinctive urge to defend Jude, despite his behaviour, and her cheeks flamed hotly as both Hadleys turned to look at her.

'How do you know?'

Predictably, it was Venetia who asked the question, and Sara put her hands behind her back, as she endeavoured to explain the situation.

'I—I'm afraid it was Harriet,' she admitted, regretting the confession, even as she said it. 'She—accidentally told your father. I think she thought he already knew.'

Rupert and Venetia exchanged glances, and then Rupert made a grateful gesture. 'I say, thanks awfully for telling me. I mean, when I spoke to Jude——'

'You already accused him?' Venetia stared impatiently at her brother.

'Well, of course,' Rupert was uncomfortable. 'I mean, Father gave me one hell of a tongue-lashing! He's practically forbidden me to ride Juniper again. And it's the Torrington Chase next week.'

'Honestly!' Venetia shook her head with evident frustration. 'Surely you realised Jude's not like that! You really are an absolute fool!'

Rupert's chin jutted. 'I don't need you to tell me that, Vennie. How do you think I feel, knowing what Father will say if he finds out about this!'

'Why should he?' Sara couldn't help the interruption. 'I mean—I'm sure Jude won't say anything, will he?'

'That's true.' Venetia took up her words. 'Here he is anyway,' she added, her face perceptibly brightening. 'You can tell him you made a mistake.'

Sara stiffened as the figure of Jude emerged from the shadow of the building. In the casual close-fitting slacks and navy jacket he had been wearing earlier, he looked so much at ease in his surroundings, and watching him descend the shallow steps towards them, Sara felt an unfamiliar prickling of her skin.

'We're back,' Venetia announced unnecessarily, going to meet him. 'Did you miss me?'

'Not particularly,' he responded, with lazy indolence, and her nose wrinkled indignantly at the careless dismissal.

'I say, Jude, I hear apologies are in order,' Rupert offered, approaching them with grudging reluctance. 'Miss Shelley here tells me it was Harriet who let the cat out of the bag, so—no hard feelings, what?'

Jude's dark lashes lifted to allow his eyes to include Sara's unwilling presence. For a moment, the grey glitter of his gaze raked her faintly discomfited countenance, and then he switched abruptly back to Rupert.

'No sweat,' he declared, flicking back his cuff to examine the watch on his wrist. 'Look, I've got to be going. I want to get back and see how Midnight's foal is doing, and Harriet's got guests coming for dinner.'

'Oh, Jude!' Venetia's lips drooped disconsolately. 'I thought we could have tea together!'

'Sorry, honey. No can do.' A wry smile softened the hard contours of his face. Then he looked deliberately at Sara. 'Are you ready to leave, too? If you are, you can come with me.'

'Oh—oh, yes,' began Sara, only to have Rupert turn to look appealingly at her.

'I say, you're not going, are you?' he protested. 'I mean, there's no need. I can run you home later. Father's tied up with his bailiff at the moment, so the three of us could have tea together.'

'I think Sara should go home,' Jude inserted flatly. 'After all, she only arrived yesterday, and she's hardly had time to get her bearings.'

'Knight's Ferry is hardly virgin territory, Jude,' Venetia put in maliciously. 'Why don't you ask Sara what she would like to do? She does have a mind of her own, when all's said and done.'

Jude's expression mirrored his impatience, but he turned obediently to Sara. 'Well?' he said. 'Do you come or do you stay?'

Sara shifted uneasily. She knew Venetia expected her to stay, if for no other reason than to confirm her earlier statement about Jude. But there was Harriet to think of, and in all honesty she had had enough of the Hadleys for one day.

'I—I think I will go with you,' she ventured, and heard Venetia's angry intake of breath. 'Thank you for your invitation,' this to Rupert, 'but I really think I've neglected Harriet long enough.'

'Well—if you insist,' said Rupert ruefully. 'But we must get together again soon.'

'I'd like that.' Sara was polite, but she was all too unhappily aware of Venetia's stormy face.

'Okay, let's go.'

Jude gestured towards the side of the house, and with an apologetic smile at the other girl, Sara fell into step beside him, raising her hand in answer to Rupert's waving farewell. Nevertheless, she was glad when they rounded the corner of the building and the Hadleys could no longer see them.

She had expected to have to walk home: it was the way she had come, after all, but to her surprise Jude led the way along the terrace to a side courtyard where the Mercedes was waiting. It was not locked, and he easily swung open the door, allowing her to lift her legs inside, before walking round to join her.

Despite her enjoyment in driving earlier, Sara found she was quite content now to let someone else take the wheel. She put it down to tiredness, refusing to admit the fact that Jude drove so much better than she did.

He didn't speak, however, and after sitting in silence for several minutes, Sara knew she had to make some attempt to retrieve a semblance of normality.

'I—I suppose an apology would be unacceptable,' she began, and he cast a chilling look in her direction.

'From me?' he demanded scornfully, and she caught her breath.

'No. From me,' she tendered stiffly. 'In spite of your behaviour, I'm prepared to admit that perhaps—perhaps you had justification——'

'How noble!' One dark brow arched satirically. 'And am I supposed to forget all about it?'

Sara held up her head. 'If we're to live in the same house, I don't see that we have much choice.'

'Don't you?' He halted at the gate that opened on to the road and half turned towards her. 'You wouldn't consider leaving, I suppose?'

Sara gasped indignantly. 'No!' She gazed tautly at him. 'Would you?'

'Unfortunately, I can't,' he retorted obscurely, and before she could ask him what he meant, he had thrust open his door and vaulted out to open the gate.

When he came back, it was difficult to broach the subject without sounding horribly inquisitive, but Sara had to say something. 'I—I suppose you mean—Harriet wouldn't want you to go,' she ventured stiffly, recalling the argument they had had the night before, and Jude's mouth assumed a sardonic slant.

'How did you guess?' he mocked, driving through the gate and jumping out to close it again. Then, as he got back into the car: 'Harriet's a very possessive lady and, as you'll find out, she likes her own way—always.'

Sara pressed her lips together. 'Well, you don't seem to worry overmuch about hurting her,' she blurted out recklessly. 'I mean, you seem to—spread yourself around——'

'Careful!' Jude was regarding her warningly, and making no immediate effort to move out into the lane, but Sara refused to be daunted:

'I couldn't help overhearing what you said to Harriet last evening, could I? About you having supper with some other female. And you can't be immune to the fact that Venetia thinks the sun shines out of you. And—and last night——'

'Yes?'

'Well, it explained why so many women think you're sexy!'

'Did it?'

With his right arm resting on the steering wheel, he was watching her intently, and Sara was not unaware of the uncertain ground she was treading.

'It did happen, didn't it?' she exclaimed. 'You can't deny that. And even though you may have had provocation, you—you took advantage of the situation.'

'How?' His left arm was along the back of her seat, and

Sara was intensely conscious of his fingers only inches from her collar.

'I—I'd rather not go into details,' she explained, checking the leather clasp that held her hair at the nape. 'I think you know what I mean. And—and I just want you to know that as far as I'm concerned it won't happen again.'

Jude rubbed the roughening skin of his jawline with a thoughtful hand, his long lashes veiling the expression in his eyes. 'And what if I don't accept that?' he probed softly. 'Are you going to tell me you objected? I seem to remember a certain eagerness to please, a hot little body, that fairly asked for everything it got!'

'Why, you—you cad!' Sara refused to use the more appropriate epithet. 'Well—well, let me tell you, I'm not here to provide you with cheap thrills!'

'Cheap thrills?' Jude's mouth parted to reveal strong white teeth. 'My God!' His mocking expression gave way to one of mild incredulity. 'You don't know much about men, do you?'

Sara bent her head. 'I don't know what you mean.'

'Then you should.' Jude's fingers suddenly gripped the swathe of hair at her nape, forcing her head up again. 'Let me tell you, what you did last night gave me no cheap thrill. On the contrary, you don't know how lucky you were. Any other man would have taken what you so generously offered!'

'I—I didn't——'

Sara lifted her hands to push his away, her heart pounding resentfully. But he moved, imprisoning her right arm against the seat with his body, and bending his head, he put his parted lips to hers.

'You *bastard*!' she choked, against his mouth, and then felt the awful weakness enveloping her as his right hand moved caressingly over her thigh. 'No—no, you mustn't,' she pleaded desperately, trying to stop him, but the persuasive pressure of his lips was seducing her resolution.

'Just to prove my point,' Jude advised a little grimly, drawing back from her with an unwilling trace of reluctance. 'Don't make promises you can't keep,' he added harshly, brushing her soft mouth with rough fingers: and Sara drew an unsteady breath as he reached lazily for the ignition.

The remainder of the journey was an anticlimax. Sara hardly dared to move, intensely conscious of his thigh only inches away from her own. Her own leg tingled, where his hand had made its sensuous exploration, and she pressed her knees together as if to dispel that traitorous weakness.

It only took a few minutes to reach Knight's Ferry, and Rob, Janet's husband, shifted his wheelbarrow out of the way as Jude parked the car in the courtyard. The old man called a pleasant greeting as they got out of the Mercedes, but Jude's response was muted, and his silver gaze impaled Sara like a sword as she turned clumsily towards the house.

Harriet met her in the hall, her brows arching in evident surprise. She looked beyond Sara enquiringly, as if waiting for someone else to materialise, but Sara, glancing over her shoulder, found that she was alone.

'I—Jude brought me home,' she offered, praying that her appearance did not betray what had happened. 'He—I believe he wanted to check on—on Midnight. I expect that's where he's gone.'

Harriet's expression did not alter. 'But why did Jude bring you home?' she demanded, and Sara saw to her surprise that the other woman was angry. 'I naturally assumed you'd stay and have tea with Venetia and her family. Do you mean to tell me you weren't invited?'

Sara caught her breath. 'I—was invited, yes,' she conceded, wondering if Harriet's anger stemmed from Jude's disappearance, or perhaps she had expected Jude to come home alone, Sara thought uneasily, and her unwanted presence had spoiled whatever plans her aunt had had. It was an ignominious position to be in, and a wave of embarrassed colour swept over her.

'Who invited you?'

Harriet seemed unaware of her discomfort, and Sara sighed. 'It was—Lord Hadley's son, actually——'

'Rupert?'

'Yes.'

'And you refused?' Harriet uttered a little scornful exclamation.

'I—well, Jude was leaving, and he offered me a lift.'

'Jude did?'

'Yes.' Sara took a deep breath. 'He—I—I thought I'd been rather selfish in leaving you for so long. And on my first day——'

Harriet's lips tightened. 'What you're saying is, Jude was behind this?'

'No, not exactly.' Remembering how Harriet had betrayed Jude's confidence earlier, Sara was loath to make any accusations. 'He agreed with me——'

'I'll bet he did!' Harriet's teeth snapped irritably. 'Oh, well, there's nothing we can do about it now.'

Sara shook her head. 'It's not important: Besides, I—I wanted to come home.'

'Did you?' Harriet's expression relaxed suddenly. 'That's a pretty compliment.'

'I meant it.' Sara didn't altogether understand Harriet's attitude, but if her aunt thought she needed companionship of her own age she would have to disabuse her. 'I'd much rather have tea with you than with the Hadleys. And besides, I don't think Lord Hadley really approved of me.'

'Don't be silly.' Just for an instant, Harriet's face showed a bitter impatience, and then she controlled it again, and tucked a friendly hand through Sara's arm. 'Come along then. We'll have tea, just as you say.' She smiled. 'You can tell me all about your trip to Buford.'

Sara nodded, but as they walked into the sitting room Harriet cast a thoughtful glance over her shoulder, as if silently promising that Jude had not heard the last of this.

CHAPTER FIVE

By the end of her first week at Knight's Ferry Sara was beginning to feel she had been brought there under false pretences. It wasn't that she was made to feel idle for not earning her keep. On the contrary, had it not been for Jude, she would have found her new life very comfortable. But the fact remained, there was nothing for her to do, and she knew herself to be the parasite she had once accused Jude of being. But what could she do? When she broached the subject of working with Harriet, she was put off with smiling excuses: 'Don't worry,' was her aunt's usual comment. 'Take it easy for a while. Enjoy your freedom. I doubt if living with your father was ever a rest cure.'

And of course, it hadn't been. Sometimes Sara had worried herself sick over where the next week's rent was coming from, but Charles Shelley had never seemed to be concerned. So long as he had enough money to play a decent game of cards, he had been content, and Sara had never dreamed he was losing the amounts he had been losing. Looking back on it now, she realised she had been unrealistic, and for this reason, if for no other, she wanted to feel her present life had a purpose.

Living at Knight's Ferry was so different from that uncertain existence. For one thing, each day had a definite pattern. And if she sometimes missed the characteristic quirks of her father's personality, that had created the peaks and chasms of their life together, the memory of his betrayal was sufficient recompense.

Of Jude himself she had seen little. During the day he was away, of course, eating breakfast in the kitchen before she was up, and not returning until late in the afternoon. On the two occasions her aunt had had guests for dinner he had remained to play host at the opposite end of the table, a dark and brooding Malvolio in his velvet dinner jacket and pleated shirt. But most other evenings he seemed to prefer other company. Not that he was always out. Janet, who despite her harsh tongue seemed to dote on him, had mentioned once or twice that he was eating in his room, and if Harriet's lips had thinned at this information, she had made no comment. If their relationship continued its stormy passage after Sara had gone to bed, she chose not to think about it, burying her head beneath the quilt and closing her ears to any verbal altercation.

Nevertheless, she did sometimes wonder whether her presence had some bearing on Jude's behaviour, but it was not something she could bring up with Harriet. Instead, she grew increasingly uneasy of her prolonged inactivity, and even considered the possibilities of asking Lord Hadley himself for employment.

She had learned through Harriet that their aristocratic neighbour was presently writing his memoirs, so perhaps he would have use for a typist, and this was one thing she had mastered. She had often typed her father's reports for him, and while her expertise would not stand professional comparison, she didn't make many mistakes. But she could hardly write to Lord Hadley without asking Harriet's advice, and besides, it might look as if she had some ulterior motive. Like wanting to work with Jude—which couldn't have been farther from the truth. But Jude was Lord Hadley's assistant. He looked after the business affairs of the estate, surely far removed from his employer's personal life, which represented the theme of his autobiography.

It was in this uncertain frame of mind that Sara

returned from a walk to the village to find Harriet waiting for her, waving a cream manilla envelope. Her aunt looked excessively pleased with herself, and Sara knew a sudden unwillingness to hear the news she was bursting to impart.

'It's an invitation,' she exclaimed, as Sara removed her waterproof coat and hung it in the cloakroom. 'From Linden Court. We're invited to a dinner party they're having on Friday evening. What do you have to say about that?'

Sara moved her shoulders in a doubtful gesture. 'Are you sure the invitation includes me?' she asked, wishing she felt more enthusiastic. 'I mean—well, I hardly know the Hadleys, do I? And actually, I've been considering asking Lord Hadley for a job.'

'Sara!' Harriet's tone was full of reproach. 'After all I've said! I've told you, I don't want you to look for employment. That's why I've given you an allowance—to give you independence.'

'Nevertheless, I do feel—useless!' Sara exclaimed, following the older woman into the library. 'Everyone else has an occupation. I can't just go on living the life of a lotus-eater!'

'Why not?' Harriet turned to her with outspread hands. 'My dear, I invited you here to be my friend—my companion. How can you possibly accomplish that task if you go out and find yourself a job?'

Sara sighed. 'Harriet, when I got your letter, I thought you wanted someone to care for you, to look after you, to do things for you that you couldn't do yourself . . .'

Harriet shook her head. 'Like what?'

'Oh——' Sara was embarrassed. 'You know.'

'I don't.' Harriet seemed determined not to make it any easier for her, and Sara was forced to improvise.

'Well—like shopping for you,' she said, avoiding any mention of changing library books, when they were surrounded with volumes of literature. 'Making meals, keeping the house tidy——'

'Walking my poodle?' enquired Harriet ironically, and Sara made a helpless gesture.

'Something like that.'

'In other words, you thought I was some decrepit old lady, in need of care and attention?' Harriet snorted incredulously. 'Sara, for heaven's sake, how old did you think I was?'

'I don't know.' Sara moved restlessly about the room. 'You know what it's like when you're a schoolgirl. You tend to think everyone over twenty-one is past it.'

Harriet nodded. 'I see. And were you terribly disappointed?'

'No!' Sara hurried to reassure her. 'I was delighted to find I'd been wrong, but——'

'You don't like it here?'

'No!' Sara gasped. 'I mean, of course I like it here. It's just—different, that's all.'

'I still need companionship, Sara,' Harriet pointed out sadly. 'Oh, Janet's a treasure and I love her dearly, but she's not family.'

Sara shrugged. 'I want to help, you know that——'

'You see, Jude can be so selfish at times,' Harriet went on, as if Sara had not spoken. 'You must have noticed how provoking he can be.'

'Well—yes——'

'He doesn't mean to be unkind, of course. It's only his way. But—well, I know I can confide in you, my dear, there are times when I think he doesn't care for me at all. And that's when I need a friend.'

Sara was appalled. She didn't know what to say. For some reason she had never anticipated being the recipient of Harriet's emotional confidences, and her conscience smote her with the reminder of her own guilt.

Harriet sniffed and pulled out her handkerchief, blowing her nose firmly before returning it to her pocket. If anything, it made Sara feel even worse, and it successfully neutralised any protest she might have been going to voice.

Instead, she shifted a little uncomfortably and said: 'If there's anything I can do——'

'I knew you'd understand, darling.' Harriet touched her shoulder with an affectionate hand. 'Your being here is a source of great happiness to me. Don't spoil it, there's a good girl!'

It wasn't until later that Sara reflected how cleverly she had been diverted from her course. By appealing to her sympathies, Harriet had successfully destroyed any hopes Sara had had of becoming self-supporting, and although she told herself that this was why she had come to Knight's Ferry, she couldn't help wishing Harriet was not so generous.

The dinner party at Linden Court provided a much-needed outlet for her thoughts. It loomed ominously two days away, and despite Harriet's reassurances Sara was not looking forward to it. Jude, it appeared, was to accompany them, a circumstance that evoked uneasy emotions of another kind, and she spent some time convincing herself that their initial hostility was no longer a complication. On the two occasions he had joined herself and her aunt for dinner, he had been unfailingly polite, speaking to her only when necessary, and treating her in much the same way as he treated Harriet's other guests. Any discomfort had been on her part, and evidently Jude was not troubled by a guilty conscience.

On Thursday morning Sara was awake early, and with the prospect of the following evening to disturb her equilibrium, she did not linger long between the sheets. It was a sunny morning, and as there had not been too many of them since her return to England, she decided to enjoy it. It only took a few minutes to wash her face and clean her teeth, and dressed in old denim jeans and a thin knitted sweater, she let herself out of her bedroom.

She was walking towards the stairs when the door to

Harriet's room opened and Jude came out. He, too, was dressed, in tight-fitting black denims and a shirt of the same material, a dark green leather jacket draped casually over one shoulder. His appearance was so sudden and unexpected, Sara had no time to think of stepping back and remaining unobserved, even had she wanted to. She was obliged to acknowledge that she had seen him, and her face flamed in hot embarrassment as she met his mocking gaze. Did he have to be so brazen about it? she thought bitterly, wishing she had waited those few extra minutes before leaving her room. It was as if he enjoyed humiliating her, and she drew an uneven breath when she realised he was waiting for her to catch up with him.

'Good morning,' he drawled, his lazy eyes missing nothing of her confusion. 'Sleep well?'

His audacity was infuriating, and Sara cast him a malevolent look. 'Very well, thank you,' she retorted tautly. 'I suppose I don't have to ask you.'

'That's very civil of you,' he remarked, allowing her to precede him down the stairs. 'I'll assume you mean I look well rested. I am. I passed a very—comfortable night.'

'Do you have to be so aggravating?' Sara exclaimed, glancing round at him angrily. 'I'm not interested in your sleeping arrangements. How you choose to dissipate your talents is no concern of mine!'

'Jealous?' he suggested in an undertone, close behind her at the bend, and she almost stumbled down the remaining steps in her eagerness to refute his claim.

'You really are despicable, aren't you?' she choked, clinging to the banister grimly, and he bowed his head in mock shame as she made it unsteadily to the hall.

However, when she would have left him there, his hand curved abruptly round her arm. 'Where are you going?'

Sara gasped. 'I don't see that that's anything to do with you!'

'It's not.' His eyes were suddenly conciliatory. 'Have

breakfast with me.'

Sara stared at him. 'I didn't get up early to have breakfast with you.'

'I know you didn't.' When he wasn't mocking her, his face was disturbingly attractive. 'But humour me, anyway. And I'll take you to see Midnight's foal after.'

Sara hesitated. 'I was going for a walk.'

'So—walk to the stables.'

'I saw the colt the morning after he was born——'

'Yes, I know.'

'And I'm sure Mr Barnes would show it to me again, if I asked him.'

'I'm sure he would.' Jude released her arm. 'I would have liked to have shown you myself, but if you insist . . .'

Sara sighed in exasperation. She was hesitating. She was actually hesitating about letting him walk her to the stables. She must be out of her mind!

'I don't eat breakfast,' she heard herself say primly, and Jude's mouth parted in a grin.

'You can always watch me eat mine,' he invited, his silver-grey eyes alight with amusement, and the temptation was almost irresistible.

Janet's eruption from the kitchen at this point effectively prevented the continuance of their conversation. She was evidently surprised to see the two young people together, but her words were the same, Sara felt sure, as they would have been had Jude been alone.

'Are ye coming for this food?' she demanded, addressing herself to him. 'It's been spoiling these five minutes past. I was just coming to call ye.'

Jude gave Sara a rueful grimace, and then turned to the old housekeeper. 'I was just suggesting that Miss Shelley might like to have breakfast with me, Janet,' he explained, 'as she's an early riser.'

'I wouldnae call seven o'clock early,' Janet retorted, sniffing contemptuously. 'And Miss Shelley doesnae eat breakfast. Nought but a slice of toast, anyway.'

Sara resented Janet's tone. It was obvious she would not welcome her in the kitchen, and some streak of perversity made her say things she would never otherwise have contemplated.

'I do like a good breakfast occasionally, Janet,' she declared sweetly. 'But if it's too much trouble . . .'

Jude's expression seemed to reveal his understanding of the situation, and Janet was not easily duped. 'It's nae trouble,' she retorted shortly, her accent thickening. 'If ye'll gae me a moment, to gae the young master his breakfast, I'll lay the table for ye.'

The young master! Sara's gaze tilted towards Jude. But he merely returned her stare blandly, and she was left feeling somewhat outmanoeuvred. The last thing she wanted was to have to wait for Janet to serve her a huge breakfast in the dining room. The open air beckoned. And besides, she wasn't hungry.

'There's no need, Janet,' she said now, half apologetically. 'Really, a cup of coffee would suffice——'

'What she means is, she'd rather eat in the kitchen with me,' Jude declared irrepressibly, and Sara's colour deepened as Janet absorbed this new development.

'T'wouldn't be fitting,' she stated at last, but Jude only scorned her assertion.

'I'm sure we can waive the formalities for once, Janet,' he told her firmly, and Sara was left with the realisation that she could not now refuse.

'Weel, if that's what ye want . . .' Janet's expression was taut with disapproval, but she disappeared through the door that led to the domestic apartments of the house without another word.

As soon as she was out of hearing, Sara sighed. 'Really, I'd much rather not,' she said, as Jude made a courtly gesture that she should follow the housekeeper. 'She doesn't want me. I'm the intruder.'

'You did impugn her capabilities,' Jude reminded her drily. Then he grinned again. 'Come on. The young master commands it!'

Sara knew she should have been angry with him for joking about something that was not funny, taken in its truest context. It was not something she cared to think about. It made her too acutely aware of his relationship with Harriet, and the irreverent attitude he adopted to that commitment. How could she even think of having breakfast with him, knowing he was as untrustworthy as he was unpredictable? And yet she could not deny his sensual attraction—and the unwilling remembrance of her own body's responses to his undoubtedly experienced advances.

With a guilty sense of betrayal she preceded him into the short corridor that led to the back of the house. To avoid being alone with him longer than was necessary, she quickened her step, and Janet looked up dourly as they entered the kitchen.

It was a huge kitchen, and Sara surmised that in the old days it had probably been cold and inefficient. But now, the stone-flagged floor had been tiled in warm, rust-coloured tiles to match the copper hoods on the split-level oven and the barbecue spit. The walls were lined with fitted units, incorporating every labour-saving device she could think of, and although the hollow of the open fire-place still remained, the chimney had been closed off and the interior lined with shelves. The heat in the room was provided by an Aga stove, and presently the room was fragrant with the smell of grilled bacon.

'Go on, sit down.' Jude nudged Sara in the back, and she stepped rather gingerly into the room to take a seat at the long pine table. Across the scrubbed board Janet was arranging a dish of porridge at a place that was already set, and Jude moved round the table to put a casual arm across the old woman's shoulders.

'You're not cross with me, are you, Janet?' he exclaimed, his expression teasing, and Janet dug him sharply in the ribs with her elbow.

'Yon mistress is nae going to like this, laddie,' she muttered, but Sara heard her, and the malicious glance that the housekeeper cast in her direction only added to her feelings of disquiet.

Jude shrugged, however, in no way put out by Janet's words. His only concession to her aggravation was to fold himself up when her elbow found its mark, moaning in mock agony as he sank into his seat.

'Och, ye've bones like rapiers, Janet!' he groaned over his porridge. 'If I didn't know better, I'd say you were trying to tell me something. What did I do to deserve this?'

Janet clicked her tongue impatiently, but she could not quite keep her unwilling amusement at bay. It was there in the suspicious brightness of her eyes and the unwary quiver of her lips, and watching them, Sara was struck once again by the deep affection between them.

It was odd, she thought, that Janet should have such a soft spot for Jude. After all, she would have expected the housekeeper to be of the old school, to whom sexual liberation was an anarchic revolution. And yet she obviously adored a man who at best was a rogue and a philanderer, and at worst a self-seeking adventurer. A man, moreover, who treated her mistress with a certain amount of contempt. It didn't make sense, particularly when Janet seemed so deeply attached to Harriet . . .

Sara abandoned her reverie as a plate of unwanted porridge was dumped unceremoniously on the table in front of her. Lukewarm and lumpy, it resembled something quite disgusting, and Sara gagged at the unwelcome comparison.

'Salt?' suggested Jude mockingly, watching her reactions. 'A good Scot always has salt with his porridge.'

Sara swallowed convulsively before speaking. 'I really don't want this,' she whispered, pushing the plate aside. 'Can't you do something?'

Jude finished his own porridge, regarding her thoughtfully. 'What would you like?' he enquired, with easy audacity, and she shook her head bitterly and turned her face away.

When Jude got up, she glanced round at him anxiously, and then saw to her relief that he had gathered both plates together. As she watched with some trepidation, he sauntered over to the sink and apparently scraped the contents of her dish down the drain.

Janet turned as what Sara realised was a sink disposal unit started up, and Jude spread his hands apologetically before resuming his seat. 'Just a little too much,' he declared, rubbing his flat stomach, but Sara knew the housekeeper had not been deceived.

The second course was more appetising, but Sara was not used to a large meal in the morning. At boarding school she had groaned over fatty bacon and watery eggs, but since she had lived with her father she had grown used to the continental style of croissants or toast. Janet's idea of a good breakfast consisted of two eggs, bacon, kidneys and sausages, with a couple of grilled tomatoes thrown in for good measure. Sara was amazed that Jude could swallow such a meal, without seeming to put on an ounce of superfluous weight.

Simply because she had to, Sara swallowed a little crispy bacon and one of the sausages. But the eggs defeated her, even firm and crisp at the edges. Instead, she drank two cups of the strong black coffee, and looked up defiantly when Jude had finished.

'Come on,' he said, pushing back his chair. 'It's too nice a morning to waste in here. See you later, Janet.'

Janet's dour expression mirrored her feelings over Sara's scarcely-touched plate, but she didn't say anything. She merely watched with her sharp eyes as Jude showed Sara the door that led into the yard at the back of the house, and the girl had no doubts that her behaviour would be reported.

'Worried?' asked Jude, sliding his arms into the jacket

he had been carrying. His lips twitched. 'Don't concern yourself over Janet. She's a crotchety old besom at the best of times.'

Sara pressed her lips together. 'That's easy for you to say.'

Jude glanced sideways at her. 'Why not for you, too?'

'Oh, she obviously thinks you're wonderful!' she muttered pushing her hands into the pockets of her jeans. 'But she doesn't like me, and she makes it obvious.'

Jude gave her a lazy grin. 'Correction, she doesn't like you being with *me*,' he declared, leading the way through the kitchen garden. 'Forget it. It doesn't matter what she thinks.'

'It does.' Sara hunched her shoulders. 'I suppose she'll tell Harriet.'

'Mmm . . . mm, probably,' he agreed carelessly. 'So what? Let her. Harriet doesn't own me.'

The words: *Doesn't she?* hovered on Sara's lips, and when she looked up and found him watching her, she knew he knew it, too.

'Relax,' he said flatly. 'I won't spoil any of Harriet's plans. Just disrupt them a little.'

Sara didn't know what he meant, but they had reached the stable yard and Mr Barnes had seen them. 'Morning, Jude—Miss Shelley!' he greeted them smilingly. 'You come to check on our newest arrival?'

'You might say that, Frank,' remarked Jude drily, glancing round at Sara. 'Where is Midnight? Still in the same place?'

'No. As a matter of fact, she and the foal are over there.' He gestured towards a small pen at the end of the stable block. 'Barry's cleaning out the stalls at the moment, and as it was such a lovely morning . . .'

'Good idea.'

Jude patted the man on the shoulder, and then he and Sara crossed the cobbled yard to where the mare was happily munching some hay, with the little colt nuzzling at her legs. A week had made a tremendous difference to the foal, and although his legs still looked scarcely capable of supporting him, he was evidently gaining strength.

Sara gasped in delight, and rested her arms on the rails of the pen. 'Isn't he adorable!' she exclaimed, forgetting her antipathy in her excitement. 'Has he got a name yet?'

'Well, we're calling him Blackie provisionally, for obvious reasons,' Jude replied wryly. 'Not very imaginative, perhaps, but his eventual registration will be as Black Knight—knight as in Knight's Ferry.'

'Oh!' Sara was pleased. 'I like that. Was Minstrel his father?'

'No.' Jude laid his arms along the rail, too, resting his chin on his knuckles. 'He was sired by a stud from another stable.' He turned his head and quirked a brow. 'Why? What do you know about such things?'

'Nothing.' Sara coloured, as he had known she would. 'I just wondered, that's all.'

'Why? Is parentage of importance to you?'

Sara pursed her lips. 'Well, of course—I mean—it matters who one's father is, doesn't it?'

'Does it?'

Sara sighed. 'Stop being so awkward! You know what I mean.'

'Do I?'

'You should.' Sara clenched her fists. 'Unless you didn't have a father,' she added sarcastically.

His expected rejoinder didn't happen. With an abrupt movement he withdrew his arms from the rail and walked away, and Sara was left with the unpleasant realisation that once again she had said something totally unforgivable.

With a guilty sense of injustice she hastened after him, catching up with him as he was about to enter the building on the opposite side of the yard. Following him inside, she realised that this was evidently the grain store, and as well as the bales of hay stacked against the walls, there were sacks piled up on the floor. Some of the sacks had burst open, however, and the clean smell of straw pervaded the atmosphere, warm and pungent, and distinctly earthy.

'Jude——'

Her tentative use of his name caused him to glance over his shoulder, but he didn't turn to look at her. 'Go find Frank,' he instructed her shortly. 'Tell him to come here, will you?'

'In a minute . . .' Sara lingered. 'Jude, what I said— well, I didn't mean to be rude.'

'Forget it.' He moved his shoulders indifferently, and crossed the floor to where a stack of bales looked definitely unsteady. 'Find Frank, there's a good girl. I want to see him.'

'Jude——'

'Oh, for God's sake!' Losing patience, he gave the pile of bales a vicious thump with his fist, and before Sara could cry a warning the whole stack tumbled down on top of him.

He went down immediately, the suddenness of the fall and the weight of the hay giving him little chance to defend himself. He disappeared beneath an avalanche of bales and a cloud of dust, and Sara didn't stop to think before launching herself into the fray.

She was on her knees tearing the hay aside when he sat up, pushing the offending bales off his legs, and gave her a rueful grimace. 'God!' he muttered, raking back his hair with a slightly unsteady hand. 'I guess I asked for that!'

'Are you all right?' Sara was red-faced and anxious, brushing scraps of hay from his sleeve, reaching to pull a straw from the unruly darkness of his hair. 'Oh, Jude, I thought they'd knocked you out!'

'Not quite,' he told her wryly. 'But thanks for your concern. It's welcome—if a little unexpected.'

Sara sat back on her heels. 'It was my fault,' she declared. 'I—I shouldn't have said what I did——'

'I told you—forget it,' he said tautly, arching one arm over his head and resting his elbow on his updrawn knee. 'Just give me a minute, will you . . .'

'Are you sure you're all right?'

Sara saw another straw lodged in the opened neckline of his shirt, and stretched her hand to take it. But to her dismay, Jude captured her fingers, and when she would have drawn them away he propelled them deliberately to his chest. His shirt had been torn open by his fall, and her fingers recoiled from the fine covering of body hair that brushed her palm.

'Touch me,' he said harshly. 'For God's sake, stop playing games!'

'I—I'm not playing games,' she breathed. 'There was a straw——'

'I know what there was,' he muttered, reaching out to take her face between his hands. 'Oh, God, come here——'

'Jude, no——' she protested, pressing her hands against him in an effort to keep him at arm's length. But all she did was lose her balance, and when she grabbed for his jacket to save her, she pulled him down on top of her.

The weight of his body knocked the breath out of her, and she lay helplessly panting for air. His chest crushed her breasts, his flanks tangled with hers in the rough bed of straw. She could feel the heat of his skin penetrating his clothes and hers, and the strong masculine scent of him in her nose and her mouth, male and intoxicating.

She thought afterwards that he had intended to pull away from her. There was a world of difference between a kiss, given and received between two upright adults, and this totally intimate embrace. He even put his hands to the floor at either side of her, as if to push himself up from her heaving body. But their eyes met and locked, hers wide and uncertain, his dark and immobile, and when he lowered his gaze to her mouth, Sara's lips parted in mute betrayal.

With a groan of anguish Jude lowered his head, his lips seeking that moist invitation. It was an involuntary reaction, his mouth hard and searching. It was as if he wanted her to fight him, and indeed Sara's hands rose to push him away from her. But beneath the soft leather of his jacket she encountered his hips, bone-hard and tautly muscled, pinning her legs to the floor. And instead of pushing him away, her hands slid over his spine, and his shuddering response set her own limbs trembling.

His mouth softened, gentled, exploring her cheeks and her eyes before returning to her lips with devastating results. As he shifted, she shifted too, fitting herself against him, yielding to his every demand, until the cool sweet air against her skin made her realise her sweater was up below her arms.

She was breathing unsteadily, quick shallow gulps of air, when the possessive pressure of his mouth allowed it, but the draught against her flesh was briefly sobering.

'No, Jude—oh, God, what are you doing?' she choked, feeling his lips encircling the tip of her breast, and his tongue probing sensually at the taut nipple.

His urgent mouth silenced her, and his hands moving caressingly over her thighs aroused in Sara an uncontrollable desire to share his exploration. Her hands found his, entwined with his, guided his with instinctive eagerness, and then were guided in their turn to the thrusting maleness she could feel against her . . .

CHAPTER SEVEN

Jude! Jude, where are you?'

The voice floated illusively on the air, not quite real, and yet not quite unreal either.

'Jude! Jude, are you in there?'

The voice was nearer now, an annoying source of irritation, and even as Sara's sexually-drugged brain struggled to comprehend its identity, Jude smothered an oath and dragged himself away from her.

'I'm here, Frank,' he said, striding swiftly to the door to intercept the other man. 'I had a bit of an accident, I'm afraid. Half the hay toppled down on me.'

'I say!' As Sara was brought abruptly to her senses, Frank Barnes uttered a shocked exclamation. She groped desperately for her sweater as he endeavoured to look over Jude's shoulder, and scrambled to her feet in an agony of shame as Jude was forced to step aside and let him see. 'I say!' he said again, but whether that was because of the mess or because he had seen Sara, she couldn't say. 'You seem to have caught it, too, Miss Shelley.'

'Yes.' Sara tried to restore her hair to some semblance of order, aware of the straw that must be everywhere clinging to her. What must the man be thinking, she thought with dismay, and what version of this story was likely to get back to Harriet?

'Let me help you.'

Barnes stepped forward to brush the revealing strands from her sleeve, and over his head Sara's eyes encountered Jude's brooding gaze. For someone who only minutes before had been dangerously close to losing control of his emotions, he was amazingly calm, but when he lifted his hands to brush the dust from his denims, she saw that they were not quite steady. Dear God, she thought, a ghost of a smile crossing her face in gratitude for Frank Barnes' assistance, if the groom had not interrupted them as he did, she might not have been able to stop him. Her knees went weak. How could he? she asked herself bitterly. How could *she*? And why did the idea of Jude possessing her body make her feel shaky, as well as ashamed?

'I'll have Barry clear this up right away.' Barnes looked round and shook his head. 'Dear me! It could have been much worse, couldn't it? You're feeling all right now, aren't you, Miss Shelley? You still look a little bit shaken.'

Sara was finding it difficult to answer him, and Jude took the question. 'She's all right,' he declared flatly. 'I took the brunt of it. But apart from a few cuts and bruises, I seem to be in one piece.' He paused. 'But you're right— it could have been worse. And I want these bales shoring up in future, and those sacks storing somewhere else.'

'Yes, sir.' Barnes adopted a conciliatory tone, his earlier familiarity giving way to mild deference. 'It's a job I've been planning on doing these weeks past, but what with Midnight foaling and Miss Ferrars sending Minstrel to Cheltenham . . .'

'I know, Frank, I know.' While Sara listened with some incredulity to this exchange, Jude gave the older man a rueful grin. 'I guess we'll say no more about this incident, hmm? You fix things up, and I'll forget it ever happened.'

Barnes nodded, and grinned in return. 'Suits me, Jude. I'm sure we can trust Miss Shelley's discretion.'

'I'm sure we can,' agreed Jude drily, and Sara walked out of the grain store on legs that were still decidedly unsteady.

Jude accompanied her to the boundary of the stable yard, and then halted. 'Are you going back to the house?' he asked, in an undertone, and she flashed him an angry look.

'What would you have me do?' she demanded, stung as much by his attitude to Barnes as by the disturbing re-membrance of what had—*and what had almost*—happened. 'I assume I'm to forget what happened in there, too, aren't I? How delightful it must be to have such an expedient conscience!'

'Sara!' His grey eyes impaled her with a savage look. 'Don't over-dramatise the situation. What happened— happened. It wasn't planned. And as God's my witness, I didn't intend for it to go as far as it did!'

'I don't suppose you did.' Sara refused to be appeased. 'After all, there's just so much one man can do, isn't there? And you have other means of expunging your frustration.'

'You think I should expunge it with you?' he demanded, flatly. 'I could, you know. Very easily. And with a great amount of satisfaction.'

Sara caught her breath. 'For you, I suppose.'

'For both of us,' he told her roughly. 'And don't pretend you don't know what I mean. You're not as innocent as all that.'

Sara bent her head. This was getting out of hand. 'I— I've never slept with a man,' she declared tautly.

'Well, obviously I can't say the same—about women, I mean,' he retorted, bringing a hot flush to her face.

'And nor do I intend to,' Sara added, forcing herself to look up at him. 'Outside of marriage, of course.'

'Really?' Jude plucked a blade of straw out of her hair, his eyes darkening disturbingly as they rested on her mouth. 'Poor old Rupert! I wonder if he knows what he's in for.'

'Rupert?' Sara gazed blankly at him. 'What has Rupert to do with it?'

'Oh—forget it.' Jude grimaced. 'It was just a thought. But how do you think you got an invitation to Linden Court?'

He swung away before Sara could question him further, striding out across the park towards Lord Hadley's home without even a backward glance. Sara was left to return to Knight's Ferry feeling bewildered, raw, and very vulnerable, unwilling to contemplate either the past or the future.

Harriet was in the library when she returned, not yet dressed, but drinking a cup of coffee, impatiently scanning the letters in the mail. She called Sara as the girl crossed the hall, and she turned back unwillingly, wishing she could have crawled in unnoticed.

'Janet tells me you went out with Jude,' Harriet remarked, without looking up from the letter she was reading.

'Yes.' Sara's tongue moistened her dry lips. 'We—er—we went to the stables. To see Midnight's foal.'

Harriet glanced up briefly. 'Where is Jude now?'

'Oh——' Sara shrugged. 'I imagine he's at Linden Court. He left me to go that way.'

'I see.' Harriet put down the letter, and regarded the girl intently. 'And you've been with him all this time?'

Sara made as if to look at her watch, realised how revealing that would be, and let her arm fall. 'Is it late?' she ventured foolishly. 'I thought it was quite early.'

'It's after nine o'clock,' replied Harriet tersely. 'Janet says you left the house before eight. Does it take the better part of an hour to look at a mare and her foal?'

Sara wanted to die. 'It—must have,' she admitted faintly. 'I'm sorry if you were anxious.'

'I'm not anxious, Sara. I'm disappointed,' Harriet retorted swiftly. 'I thought we were friends. I thought we had respect for one another.'

'We do——'

'Do we?' Harriet's lips tightened. 'When you return from the stables with straw on your garments and your hair all mussed, I'm to believe you've just been examining a mare and its foal?'

Sara bent her head. 'I'm sorry.'

Harriet sniffed. 'So—what have you been doing?'

'I—fell,' said Sara lamely. 'In—in the stables.' She touched her hair. 'I didn't realise it was so—so——'

'Obvious?' suggested Harriet shortly. 'Really, Sara, you can't expect me to believe your appearance is the result of a *fall*!'

Sara shook her head. 'I did fall,' she insisted. At least that was true. What came after, she could not reveal, not even if Harriet refused to speak to her again.

'Very well.' The other woman heaved a heavy sigh. 'I suppose I must accept that you choose not to be honest with me——'

'That's not true——'

'What is true, Sara?' Harriet bit off the words. Then, suddenly, she spread her hands. 'Oh, very well. What's the use of us arguing? I don't like hostility, Sara, I never have, and if a little thing like this can cause so much dissent, I suggest we forget it.'

'Harriet——'

'Please.' Her aunt held up her hand. 'Let's say no more about it. I shall speak to Jude myself when he returns.'

Sara felt terrible. 'Can—can I go and tidy myself up now?' she asked unhappily, as Harriet returned to her mail, and the older woman shrugged.

'Why not? You haven't forgotten that the vicar and his wife are coming for coffee this morning, have you? I shouldn't like them to see you in that state.'

Sara had forgotten, but she nodded her head a little jerkily before beating a hasty retreat to the sanctuary of her bedroom. She intended to take a shower. To scrub away every trace of Jude's lovemaking from her body; until these awful feelings of guilt and betrayal were erased once and for all.

Sara did not see Jude again that day. The weather had changed in concert with her mood, and when she went down for dinner it was raining quite heavily, the sky low and overcast, casting shadows in the corners of the library.

'Put on the light, darling,' Harriet instructed from the depths of the couch, when Sara came in at the door, but once again the switch refused to work.

'Oh, leave it.' Harriet lifted her hand and pressed the switch on the lamp nearest to her. 'Now try it,' she added, and Sara did, her eyes widening in surprise when the lamps were illuminated. 'It's these old houses,' Harriet explained, inviting her to help herself to a drink. 'The wiring is slightly old-fashioned. Two-way switches meant something different to them. If the light is turned off at the door, it needs to be turned on at the door. Likewise with the lamps.'

'So if I turned the switch at the door, I could prevent you from turning on the lamp,' Sara tendered.

'Something like that,' Harriet agreed comfortably. 'Now come and sit down, darling. I have an apology to make.'

'An apology?' Sara's fingers stiffened round her glass.

'Yes. Oh, do sit down. Stop hovering, dear. Jude's told me what actually happened this morning.'

'He has?' Sara was appalled. 'Oh, Harriet——'

'Silly girl! Thinking you had to protect Barnes! I've promised Jude I won't say a word, even though he was responsible.'

Sara slumped back against the buttoned upholstery. 'I see.'

'Naturally, if you'd told me you'd been knocked down by a stack of bales, I'd have understood your dishevelled appearance. Instead of which you let me think Jude had tumbled you in the hay.'

Sara's hot cheeks merely confirmed Harriet's opinion. She thought she had embarrassed her, talking about such things. The truth was, Sara was mortified with shame.

'Harriet——'

'Not another word.' Harriet squeezed her arm affectionately. 'I must learn not to jump to conclusions. Now, you can tell me what you're planning to wear tomorrow evening.'

By the time the following evening arrived Sara was a veritable bundle of nerves. After what Jude had said, and her uneasy reconciliation with Harriet, she should have felt more relaxed, but she didn't. She was taut and apprehensive, aware that several pairs of eyes would be upon her, not least those of Venetia, and Jude himself, of course.

Harriet had approved what she was wearing: a floaty creation in ice-green chiffon, with a cape-like neckline falling in transparent folds over her shoulders. It was a simple style, but very effective, and with her hair loose for once, she knew she would not let Harriet down. If only Jude was not going to be there, she wished fervently, and came down the stairs to find just such an argument going on.

'You can't let me down, Jude. I won't let you!' Harriet's voice carried through the half open door of the sitting room. 'How can I pretend you're not well enough to come with us, when you were with James less than three hours ago!'

'I'd just rather not be there, that's all,' Jude retorted harshly. 'For God's sake, why do you need me? You can prepare the sacrifice equally well alone!'

'Jude, I will not have this kind of talk from you. After all I've done for you, the least you can do is show a little appreciation.'

Sara hung back at the foot of the stairs, not wanting to eavesdrop, yet incapable of closing her ears to their exchange. It wasn't exactly flattering to hear of Jude's aversion for her company, and what sacrifice was he talking about? She didn't begin to understand.

The sound of a door opening behind her alerted her to Janet's presence, and she quickly deserted her post to walk determinedly into the sitting room. The last thing she wanted was for the housekeeper to add spying to her list of faults. Her relationship with Harriet was not yet strong enough to stand that kind of strain.

Harriet was standing on the hearth at her entrance, a slim sophisticated figure, in a plain black gown that complemented her chestnut hair. Jude, meanwhile, was lodged in an armchair, one leg thrown carelessly over the arm, a dark and disturbing antagonist, in matching black velvet.

'Oh, there you are, dear.' Harriet spoke with evident

relief as Sara entered the room, and Jude rather reluctantly got up from the chair. 'You look beautiful,' she
added, glancing round at her companion. 'Doesn't she,
Jude? Aren't you proud to have two such elegant ladies to
escort?'

'Oh, indeed.' But Jude's tone was flat. 'Well, shall we
go? Before I say something we'll all regret.'

'The car's at the door, Miss Ferrars,' Janet's voice announced from the doorway. 'What time shall I ask Rob
to come back for you?'

'Oh——' Harriet started to speak, but Jude's words
overrode her. 'There's no need for Rob to turn out, Janet,'
he declared, ignoring Harriet's instinctive protest. 'I'll be
driving the ladies myself, and I'll bring them back when
they want to come.'

'But, Jude, you know how foolish it is to drink and
drive——'

'Who's drinking?' Jude spread his hands towards her.
'Cool down, Harriet, it's only a matter of three miles or
so on quiet roads. I'm not exactly an inebriate!'

'But on these occasions——'

'Oh, I know.' Jude's lips twisted bitterly. 'I have been
known to drown my boredom in alcohol. But you can
always walk home, if you don't trust me.'

They stared at one another angrily, grey eyes gazing
into brown, and Sara shifted a little uncomfortably. She
had the disturbing feeling that if she and Janet had not
been there, their antagonism would have erupted in real
violence, but what form that violence might have taken,
she didn't care to contemplate.

'Oh, very well.' Harriet gave in, bending to pick up
her sequinned evening bag before preceding them out of
the room. 'Jude will drive us, Janet, thank you. I'll explain
the position to Rob, when we get to the car.'

Sara collected her leather coat from the hall cloakroom
on their way out, and flinched when Jude took it from
her, and held it for her to put on. She thought his hands

lingered longer than was necessary on her shoulders, after
she had slid her arms inside, but she might have been
mistaken and could hardly accuse him anyway. Nevertheless, she moved ahead of him rather quickly, reaching
the car before he did, and gasping in surprise at its unexpected luxury.

It was a Rolls-Royce, not a new one, it had to be said,
but in superb condition. Chrome and paintwork gleamed
in the approaching dusk, and inside the leather shone like
new.

'It was my father's,' Harriet exclaimed, after explaining
the situation to Rob. 'We only use it on special occasions.'
She took Jude's hand to help her into the front seat. 'But
tonight is a special occasion, isn't it? Our first dinner at
Linden Court together.'

Jude's mouth turned down at the corners, but he swung
open the rear door for Sara to get in, and slammed it
firmly behind her, before walking round to take the wheel.
Then, with a wave of farewell for Janet, he set the old car
in motion, and they moved majestically down the drive
towards the gates.

Linden Court looked different at night. Although it was
not yet dark, lights gleamed from many windows, not
just those of the family wing. There were other cars
too, parked on the drive, and in the private courtyard,
where Jude parked the Rolls, and Sara's mouth dried
up altogether as she anticipated the evening ahead of
her.

A maid took their coats in the entrance hall, her smile
for Jude eloquent of their shared employment. 'His lordship and his guests are in the drawing room, Miss Ferrars,'
she declared, folding Harriet's cape over her arm. 'I'm
sure you know the way.'

'Thank you, Vera.' Harriet acknowledged the girl's
directions. 'And how is your mother these days? I really
must come and see her.'

'I'm sure she'd be delighted, miss,' Vera exclaimed

gratefully. 'Being on her own so much, she does get kind of lonely. It's not much fun being in a wheelchair. I hope it never happens to me.'

'I'm sure we all hope that, Vera,' Harriet said sympathetically, but the look Jude gave her was impatient.

'Your mother's illness is not hereditary, Vera,' he put in drily. 'There's no earthly reason why you should develop her symptoms. Now, if you'll excuse us . . .'

Harriet gave him a killing look before preceding him through an open archway into a wide corridor. At the end, open doors revealed a colourful gathering of people, all talking and laughing and having drinks, and Sara stiffened selfconsciously as their approach was noticed.

'I wish you wouldn't interrupt when I'm talking to the servants, Jude,' Harriet snapped in an undertone, her fixed smile a travesty of the emotions she was suppressing.

'And I wish you wouldn't treat Vera as if she was some kind of mental defective,' retorted Jude bleakly. 'Her mother has a bone marrow deficiency,' he explained for Sara's benefit. 'The poor girl worries enough, without Harriet putting doubts into her mind.'

'I did not do that!'

'I'm sure we all hope that,' Jude mimicked brutally, and Harriet's breathing quickened as they reached the entrance to the drawing room.

Although the room had seemed to be full of people, Sara saw to her relief that there were perhaps only a dozen other guests. But although the room was huge, they were all grouped together round Lord Hadley, who was holding forth on the subject of fox-hunting, and in consequence there had seemed to be more.

The room itself was magnificent. The ceiling was carved and fluted, the walls were tall, and covered in paintings, and the furniture matched its surroundings. There were a number of sofas, upholstered in figured cream damask; several easy chairs, some with arms, some without; and many polished tables and cabinets, holding articles of evident value. It was the kind of room Sara had hitherto only seen from a public gallery, and the differences between Knight's Ferry and Linden Court were now becoming more apparent.

Their host saw them at once, and with innate courtesy he abandoned his story to come and greet them. But Rupert forestalled him, having glimpsed their approach along the corridor, and it was his hand that reached first for Sara's, and the warmth of his welcome that enveloped her.

'I say, you look stunning!' he exclaimed, raising her fingers gallantly to his lips. 'And you, too, Miss Ferrars,' he added, as an afterthought. 'You both look wonderful!'

Harriet evidently didn't mind Rupert's preference. 'It's so nice to hear real old-fashioned compliments,' she declared, as Lord Hadley joined them. 'Isn't that so, James? Your son does you credit.'

Lord Hadley glanced at Jude first, then at Rupert, before finally bringing his attention to Sara. 'What do you think, my dear?' he enquired crisply. 'As the only objective person present, what is your verdict?'

'Oh, I'm sure the son is only a reflection of the father,' she murmured, not consciously seeking his approval, and heard Jude make a derisive sound behind her.

'Well, you can't say fairer than that,' remarked Lord Hadley drily, and Sara saw Harriet's smile of approval, as he took her to find a drink and meet his guests.

The first person Sara recognised was Venetia, standing with another girl of similar appearance. They were both smaller than Sara, but the unknown girl was of daintier proportions than Rupert's sister. Venetia was wearing a beautifully designed dress of Indian silk, but once again its full-skirted cut accentuated her hipline, while her companion's gown of stiffened damask would have suited a more generous figure.

Venetia's expression was not friendly, and she turned and said something to the girl beside her that caused them both to snigger. But Venetia's animosity was not her problem, and Sara endeavoured to remember names as Lord Hadley made his introductions.

'Your father was Charles Shelley, the journalist, wasn't he?' one beetle-browed old colonel enquired sharply. 'Damn fine columnist. A shame he had to die like that.'

'Thank you.'

Sara was grateful, but the colonel hadn't finished. 'Got any leanings in that direction yourself?' he persisted, when Lord Hadley would have drawn her away. 'Own a couple of papers hereabouts. Could do with some fresh blood, what?'

'I don't think Miss Shelley is looking for a job, Colonel,' Rupert Hadley remarked behind them. 'Father, Calder is looking for you. I think he wants to let you know that dinner is ready.'

Lord Hadley looked distinctly put out by the interruption, but he had little choice other than to go and speak to Calder, whoever that was. However, he had one thing to say before he left them:

'You won't forget you're taking Elizabeth in to dinner, will you, Rupert?' The warning in his voice was unmistakable. 'Introduce Peter to Sara: he's dying to meet her.'

'Yes, Father.' Rupert's response was polite, but as soon as his father was out of earshot, he gave Sara a rueful grin. 'Orders is orders,' he grimaced, his palm cupping her elbow. 'But when dinner is over, I'd like to show you around.'

'Well, that's very kind of you——'

Sara didn't know what to say, but Rupert was appealingly enthusiastic. 'It's not polite at all,' he admitted, speaking in a low voice. 'I've been looking forward to meeting you again. And when Miss Ferrars suggested this dinner party——'

'Harriet suggested this dinner party?' Sara interrupted him disbelievingly, but Rupert merely squeezed her arm.

'It's all right. Father was delighted to arrange it. It's quite usual to have a party to introduce new people.'

'Yes, but—Harriet's had dinner parties——'

'This is different,' said Rupert confidently. 'Oh, don't look like that. Miss Ferrars and my father are old friends. They go—oh, way back. Before either Venetia or I was born, actually.'

'And—and your mother?'

'Didn't you know? Mother died soon after Venetia was born. Father's been a widower for almost twenty years.'

'Has he?'

Sara was confused, and it didn't help to be introduced to yet another strange young man, whose quiff of reddish hair and rather effeminate appearance combined to give him a foppish air.

'This is Peter Hedgecomb,' Rupert explained. 'Peter, meet Sara. And now, I've got to go and look after Elizabeth, while you take the most beautiful girl in the room in to dinner!'

'My pleasure,' said Peter Hedgecomb chivalrously. 'Can I get you another drink, Sara? Your champagne appears to have got rather flat.'

Dinner was eventually served in the small dining room. Sara only knew it was the small dining room because Peter Hedgecomb told her so. She couldn't imagine the size of the large dining room if this was the small one, and she used her interest in her surroundings to give her time to assimilate what she had learned.

It didn't make sense that Harriet should ask Lord Hadley to give a dinner party for *her*! And besides, she had not realised he and Harriet were so close. Remembering Lord Hadley's attitude on the occasion of their first meeting, she could not believe his decision had been a spontaneous one, but why had he allowed himself to be persuaded? Was this what Jude had meant when he spoke about a sacrifice? But whose sacrifice? And for what purpose?

The meal might have been sawdust for all the enjoyment she took from it. The fourteen participants were seated around a long refectory table, and Sara noticed that Rupert's partner was the girl who had been standing with Venetia earlier. Venetia herself was seated between another youngish man and Jude, with Harriet on his other side. And it was to Jude that Venetia addressed herself almost exclusively, so that watching him across the candlelit table, Sara knew a troubling sense of irritation. She wasn't jealous! She *couldn't* be, she told herself severely. But when Jude bent his head towards Venetia, and her gurgling laugh broke out, a bitter feeling of injustice stirred inside her.

They were served soup, and fish in a creamy sauce, poultry cooked in wine, and a delightful raspberry soufflé. The soup went down easily, and the fish literally melted in Sara's mouth, but she had a little trouble with the duckling, and the tiny new potatoes and varied choice of vegetables defeated her. Ignoring Jude's mocking gaze as she refused first one tray and then another, she managed to swallow a little of the dark flesh, washing it down liberally with half a glass of red wine.

As they ate, the portraits of long-dead Hadleys looked down on them, and over the massive screened fireplace the coat of arms was repeated, together with a pair of crossed swords. Fortunately, the heating was not as old as the suit of armour, that stood incongruously in one corner of the room, and the light from the candelabra was kind to its faded glory.

Sara half expected the female members of the party to retire alone after dinner, leaving the men to their port, as was usual in days gone by. But Lord Hadley and his guests all left the table together, adjourning to the drawing room, where coffee and brandy were waiting.

Sara refused the brandy Peter Hedgecomb offered her, but took the seat he indicated on the sofa. Then, while he was getting their coffee, she glanced about her, looking away abruptly when Harriet caught her eye.

'I hope Peter's been taking good care of you, Sara.' Venetia's faintly scornful voice made her look up. 'I think you should know Rupert's practically engaged to Elizabeth, so it's no use casting your eyes in his direction.'

Sara kept her temper with an effort, but right now she had other things on her mind. 'What's the matter, Venetia?' she asked pleasantly. 'Can't you stand the competition?'

Venetia sucked in her breath. 'How dare you?'

'How dare you?' countered Sara tranquilly. 'Your brother's old enough to speak for himself, isn't he? And besides, I'm not looking for a husband.'

'Then why did Harriet arrange this dinner party? She did arrange it, you know. Daddy would never have thought of it himself.'

'I know that.' Sara was at least glad she had not had to hear the news from Venetia. 'I suppose she thought she was doing me a favour.'

'She knew how Rupert would react,' retorted Venetia hotly. 'She knows Daddy's been trying for months to get him to propose to Elizabeth. So she deliberately throws you into his path, to complicate the issue.'

Sara was going to object, but there was a certain amount of logic in what Venetia was saying. Had that been Harriet's objective? To throw her and Rupert together? And was that why Jude had been so scathing about their invitation to Linden Court?

It was all beginning to make sense, except that she had no desire to get involved with Rupert Hadley. She liked him—what she knew of him anyway—but he didn't attract her sexually. Unlike Jude, her conscience pricked her mockingly.

'Anyway, I just thought I'd put the record straight,' Venetia added, smoothing the sleeves of her dress. 'And surprise, surprise—here comes my brother. Exactly on cue, as usual.'

Rupert gave both girls a curious look. Then he turned to Sara. 'Ready for the grand tour?' he asked, holding out a hand to pull her up from the sofa. 'I think we'll start in the library. We've got an illustrated manuscript, I think you'd like to see.'

'Grand tour?' Venetia said the words sarcastically, and Sara sighed as she let Rupert bring her to her feet.

'Your brother has kindly offered to show me round the house,' she declared flatly. 'You can come with us, if you like. I don't mind.'

'Well, I do,' exclaimed Rupert indignantly. 'Mind your own business, there's a love, Venetia. I don't interfere when you go chasing Jude all over the building.'

'I do not chase Jude,' Venetia flared angrily. 'He doesn't object, anyway.'

'That's not been my interpretation,' said Rupert, with airy confidence. 'Go take a powder, will you? I want to talk to Sara.'

'What about Elizabeth?' demanded his sister. 'Don't you think you owe her something?'

'I think I'll owe you a lot more, if you don't keep your opinions to yourself,' Rupert said emphatically.

'Here's Peter. What are you going to say to him?' Venetia persisted, and Sara took the cup of coffee he had brought her with some relief.

'Your father was looking for you, Rupe,' he remarked, sipping from his own cup, and Venetia chuckled maliciously as her brother cast an impatient look in Lord Hadley's direction.

'Look, I think we should leave the tour for another time,' Sara ventured ruefully. 'I mean, you shouldn't abandon your guests, and if your fiancée——'

'I have no fiancée,' Rupert asserted grimly, giving his sister a savage look. 'But okay, maybe this isn't the best time to get together.' He found her hand and turned her so that they were both facing away from the others. 'I'll ring you,' he mouthed, squeezing her fingers, and before she could say anything in reply, he walked away.

Venetia met Sara's gaze with a challenging stare, but after a few moments she shrugged, as if abandoning any further efforts to direct her brother's life. 'Where's Jude?' she murmured, half to herself, and moved away to find him, leaving Sara and Peter alone.

'Enjoying yourself?' he asked, putting a slim cheroot between his teeth, and Sara knew an hysterical desire to laugh.

'Oh, yes,' she said, and she could hear the suppressed emotion causing her voice to rise. 'It's been—quite fascinating,' she averred, putting down her coffee cup, and Peter accepted her answer, as if it was exactly what he had expected.

CHAPTER EIGHT

HARRIET came to find her at ten-thirty, and Sara, steeling herself to meet the older woman's censure, found her aunt distressed over an entirely different matter.

'Where's Jude?' she exclaimed. 'Have you seen him? He was with Venetia earlier, and now they've both disappeared.'

Sara's stomach plunged. 'How—how should I know where they are?' she replied tautly, and although Harriet was evidently upset she noticed the deliberate challenge.

'Is something the matter, Sara?' she asked, taking time out to probe this new development, but the girl only shook her head and didn't answer.

'They may be in the library, Miss Ferrars,' Peter suggested from his seat on the arm of Sara's chair. 'It's Venetia's usual place, if you know what I mean. And of course Jude knows it, too.'

'Yes. Yes, thank you, Peter.' Harriet paused only long

enough to give Sara another puzzled look, before charging away across the floor, her usually calm façade in
tatters.

'Poor old Jude,' remarked Peter, after she had gone.
'Imagine living with someone as possessive as her! No
wonder she keeps such a tight rein on him. She'd never
control him otherwise.'

Sara gazed up at him. 'And doesn't she have a right to
be possessive!' she exclaimed.

'Oh, yes. Yes, I guess so.' Peter shrugged. 'It's a pity
she never married. I guess that's the only way he's going
to get his freedom.'

Sara was appalled. Did everyone know what was going
on? And how could they sympathise with Jude, when it
was Harriet who deserved their compassion? Was it really
a case of the woman always bearing the blame, particularly a woman who was so much older than her lover?
Her lover!

Sara felt sick. She had tried not to think of this aspect
of their relationship, but how could she help it when Harriet showed so blatantly how much she depended upon
him—had she no shame? Didn't she care that these people
might be laughing at her, deriding their affair, and ridi-
culing her part in it?

Jude had no shame, that was obvious. He knew how
Venetia felt about him. He couldn't fail to be aware of
her infatuation. And yet he deliberately encouraged it,
knowing her father objected, and hurting Harriet indis-
criminately.

Sara's own feelings towards her aunt underwent an
abrupt reversal. After all, why should she feel angry with
Harriet for trying to throw her and Rupert together, if
that really was what she had intended? It was not
something to be ashamed of. She was only thinking of
her, of her future; and she was mistress of her own destiny,
wasn't she? She didn't *have* to do anything she didn't want
to. And she should be flattered to think that Lord Hadley's

son was attracted to her.

'Excuse me.'

Peter got up at that moment to go and find another drink, and in his absence Sara lifted an unsteady hand to her hair. What an evening, she thought wryly, and what a revelation it had been.

'All alone?'

The challenge was unexpected, its deliverer more so, and Sara glanced up at Jude in surprise. 'What are you doing here?' she exclaimed, recalling Harriet's unseemly exit, and wondering with some confusion how she ever could have missed him.

'I'm a guest—remember?' he retorted, hands pushed deep into the pockets of his jacket. 'Where's the Honourable Peter? Or have you ditched him—just to please Harriet, of course.'

The irony in his tone was unmistakable, and Sara gave him a frosty look. 'I don't know what you mean,' she informed him coldly. 'Perhaps you should know that Harriet is looking for you. Apparently she's upset by your cavalier attitude!'

'My what!' Jude suppressed an infuriating laugh. 'Dear me, do people really still use that word?' He sobered. 'What am I supposed to have done? Fought a duel with Rupert over my lady's favour?'

'You know perfectly well I mean,' exclaimed Sara, wishing she was standing, and not being forced to look up at him. 'Harriet thinks you're with Venetia.' She paused, her nails biting into her palms. 'You wouldn't expect her to be pleased about it, would you?'

'No.' Jude shrugged. 'No, I guess not.'

'How can you stand there and speak so casually about something that should arouse some sense of conscience?' Sara gasped. 'You may not care, but you could consider Harriet's feelings!'

'Why should I? When did she ever consider mine?' enquired Jude, his brief amusement disappearing. 'For

God's sake, Sara, what do you think I've done? Raped the girl? I think James's hounds would have had some objection to make about that!'

Sara caught her breath, pushing herself up out of the chair. 'You admit—you have been with Venetia, then?'

'We've been talking, yes.' Jude was unrepentant. 'Why shouldn't I talk to her? Do you have any objections?'

'Me?'

Sara looked past him coldly, unable to meet the challenging hostility in his eyes, and saw Harriet and Venetia just entering the room.

Harriet seemed somewhat harassed, her usually calm features drawn into stiff lines, while Venetia looked as if she had been crying, hardly an optimistic augury for the future. Sara hesitated, unsure now whether to go to Harriet or not. Sara's own earlier frustration seemed a small thing compared to the humiliation Harriet must be suffering, but before she could move, Jude's fingers had curved about her wrist.

'Let's go,' he said, and she turned to look at him incredulously. 'We're not wanted here. Or at least, I'm not. Come home with me now, before Harriet gets her second wind.'

Sara choked back a sob, dragging her hand angrily from his grasp. 'How can you?' she cried. 'How can you be so callous? Those two women love you! Doesn't that mean anything to you?'

'Not what it means to you, obviously,' retorted Jude grimly. He shook his head. 'You're a born victim, aren't you, Sara? You see the web, but you still step into it.'

Sara ignored him, pressing her hands together, staring across the room to where Harriet and Venetia had been joined by Lord Hadley. What were they saying? she wondered. At least Harriet had an ally in the girl's father, if what Venetia had said was true.

'Let me know when your particular trap begins to close, will you?' Jude murmured in a low voice, his lips almost brushing her ear. And as she jerked her head away in confusion, he left her to face her aunt alone.

Peter returned before Harriet could make her way across the room to where Sara was waiting. 'Is something wrong?' he asked, noticing her tense face and following the direction of her gaze. 'What's going on? Didn't I see Jude with you just now?'

'What? Oh—oh, yes.' Sara was half impatient. She shook her head. 'Nothing's wrong. I—er—I just think perhaps it's time I was leaving.'

'Oh, no!' Peter swallowed a gulp of champagne in disgust. 'I say, you're not going yet. You can't. I—well, it's too early. I'll drive you home later. If Harriet wants to leave, let her. The night's still young.'

'Thank you, but I shall be going with Harriet,' declared Sara firmly, biting her lip. 'I—er—I've enjoyed talking to you, but——'

'—but you're leaving,' finished Peter gloomily. 'Isn't that the story of my life!'

Sara managed a faint smile, but half to her relief, she saw Harriet approaching. 'Where's Jude gone now?' the older woman demanded, the taut lines of her face making her look older than Sara had ever seen her. 'Didn't you tell him I was looking for him? Really, Sara, I should have expected you to show that courtesy!'

'I told him. Of course I told him.' Sara was embarrassed, aware of Peter's faintly jaundiced eye. 'I don't know where he is. He—he just disappeared.'

'In a puff of smoke, what!' Peter chuckled, but sobered at the killing contempt in Harriets gaze.

'I suppose he may have gone home,' Harriet reflected grimly. 'It's like him—to walk out and leave me to make the explanations.'

Sara sighed. 'Shouldn't we go home, too?' she suggested gently. 'After all, it is late, and—well, I'm ready.'

'Are you?' Harriet's eyes flickered over her critically. 'And have you enjoyed yourself?'

Sara glanced awkwardly at Peter. 'Of course.'

'Hmm.' Harriet did not sound convinced. 'Oh, very well, let's go.' And as they walked across the floor: 'What happened to Rupert? I thought he was going to show you the house.'

Sara wondered how Harriet had discovered that, but she merely shrugged her shoulders. 'His father kept him busy,' she said indifferently, wishing she had only Rupert to worry about. 'He told me *you* arranged this party. Why did you pretend the invitation came from his father? I—well, I was terribly embarrassed.'

'Not here, Sara.'

Harriet cut her off abruptly, leaving the girl to make her farewells, and Sara stood awkwardly waiting for her to return. She managed to convey her own goodbyes by the means of a smile, but it stiffened somewhat when Rupert came up to speak to her.

'I'll phone tomorrow,' he said, taking both her rather limp hands in his and squeezing them tightly.

Sara shook her head. 'Not—not tomorrow,' she protested, unable at the moment to face the prospect of meeting any of the Hadleys again. 'Give me a couple of days. I—I feel as if I've got a migraine coming on.'

'Oh, poor Sara!' Rupert was sympathetic. 'Is there anything I can do? Anything you need?'

'No. No, nothing, thank you.' Sara forced a smile, and as she did so, Harriet came back.

The older woman's eyes flashed speculatively as she took in their apparent intimacy, and Sara withdrew her hands at once, putting them behind her back.

'Goodnight, Rupert,' said Harriet, her feelings evidently mollified by this display of attention. 'It's been quite an evening. Will we be seeing you in the near future?'

Sara cringed, but Rupert was enthusiastic. 'In the *very* near future,' he promised, looking pleased with himself, and Harriet's expression softened in satisfaction as they went to collect their coats.

The Rolls-Royce was standing where they had left it, but there was no sign of Jude. Sara had wondered whether they might find him waiting in the car, but apparently, if he had left, he had made his way home across the park. She wondered if Harriet had a spare set of keys as her aunt opened the door, but then saw in the light from the courtesy bulb that the keys were hanging in the ignition.

Harriet made a sound of impatience and then indicated that Sara should drive. 'Isn't this just typical?' she exclaimed, wrenching open the passenger side door and getting inside out of the cold night air. 'He dismisses Rob, and then leaves us to drive ourselves home!'

'He could have taken the car,' remarked Sara provocatively, her temper still simmering from that earlier setdown, but Harriet only snorted as she settled into her seat.

There was no alternative but that Sara should drive, and she reflected rather bitterly that perhaps for once she was to earn her keep. Although driving a stately limousine some three or four miles could hardly count in that capacity.

'He knew what I'd have to say to him when I saw him,' Harriet continued, as Sara adjusted the seat to suit her own height. 'He's made a complete fool of me! I don't know when I have been more angry.'

Sara moistened her dry lips. 'I was angry, too, Harriet. As it happened, Rupert told me you'd asked his father to arrange this party, but it could just as easily have been Venetia. Why did you do it? I just don't understand.'

Harriet sniffed. 'James was happy to do it. Besides, he owes me a favour. Why shouldn't I want the best for you? You are my—niece, after all.'

'But we've had dinner parties at Knight's Ferry,' Sara protested, the car's headlights picking out the curving sweep of the drive. 'Why couldn't we have had the party there? If—if you felt it was necessary.'

Harriet sighed. 'I wanted you to see Linden Court.'

'I saw Linden Court, the day you took me up there to meet Lord Hadley,' Sara reminded her tensely, and Harriet made a sound of impatience.

'You must realise that the Hadleys can command a different kind of gathering. I mean—I know the people they associate with, I'm very friendly with them, but I don't get invited to their dinner parties and they wouldn't come to mine.'

Sara cast a startled look at her. 'Does that matter?'

'Of course it matters.' Harriet was irritable. 'Honestly, Sara, are you deliberately trying to provoke me?'

'No——'

'Then for goodness' sake, girl, think sensibly! I wanted you to meet the kind of people the Hadleys associate with. I wanted them to see you in that company. I wanted them to realise how infinitely more suited you are to mix with their set, than—well, than others I could mention.'

Sara shook her head. She was remembering what Venetia had said, what she had accused Harriet of doing. But Sara wouldn't accept that this was true. She didn't *want* to accept it.

'I appreciate your confidence in me, of course,' she said, seeking an escape. 'But I don't see that it matters what the Hadleys and their friends think of me.'

'I—*care*—what the Hadleys think,' declared Harriet, between her teeth. 'Isn't that sufficient reason for you?'

Sara could feel a distinct throbbing in her temples now. She was getting the headache she had invented for Rupert's benefit. It seemed as if whatever way she turned, she came up with the same suspicion. Harriet did have hopes that Rupert might find her niece attractive, more attractive than the girl his father had approved for him. Venetia could be right. And even Jude, with his talk of lambs and sacrifices, might have been trying to warn her.

Jude! Her fingers tightened on the wheel. He had no cause to criticise Harriet, or indeed anything she did. His own behaviour left a lot to be desired, and without his intervention in her life, Harriet might never have become involved with the Hadleys. It was all his fault really, Sara thought resentfully. He was completely without scruple.

When she got out of the car to open the gate that led on to the public road, the cold air struck her like a knife. Shivering, she tugged the gate open, and then climbed back into the car to drive it through. It was bigger than the Porsche, much longer for one thing, and it jutted dangerously into the road when she attempted to leave it while she closed the gate. It could be a hazard in the dark, and sighing, she drove out on to the road, leaving the engine running, while she ran back to close the gate. As she did so, the headlights of another vehicle swept the narrow lane. It was coming fast, accelerating down the bank, and Sara had only time to fling herself out of its path before it struck the stationary Rolls. There was a horrible grinding of metal on metal, sparks flew as the car's headlights exploded on impact, and then the ominous sound of a car horn, as if a body had been thrown across a steering wheel.

The horn had an eerie sound, its persistent tone ringing in Sara's ears as she scrambled out of the ditch that had saved her from certain extinction. It was like a death knell, and her heart pounded unsteadily as she got to her feet and lurched towards the two cars. The Rolls-Royce's headlights were still working, giving a ghostly illumination to the scene, the steam rising from the smashed radiator of the other car drifting like a wraith over the bonnet.

'Harriet!' Her aunt's name spilled from her lips, softly at first, and then more forcefully, as fear and apprehension brought panic rising to the surface. 'Harriet! Harriet, are you all right? Oh, God, please don't let her be seriously injured!'

The sound of a groan reached her ears as she groped her way past the vehicle that had collided with the Rolls, and briefly she hesitated. She was not consciously trying to put off the moment when she must see for herself whether Harriet had been hurt, but there was a certain relief in the momentary delay.

The bonnet of the car was a crumpled mess, concertinaed like so much scrap metal, but as her eyes adjusted themselves to the darkness, she saw there was a man behind the wheel who was evidently not unconscious. He was shifting about and it was his groans she could hear, and she saw to her relief that he was alone in the vehicle.

But Harriet deserved her first consideration, and ignoring the man's patent pleas for assistance, Sara groped her way on to where her aunt was slumped in the front of the Rolls. It was difficult to see, but with the help of the interior light she was able to discern that Harriet was unconscious, and the blood streaming from the cut on her forehead was evidence enough of the cause.

Harriet had slumped sideways after the accident, but as Sara opened the door she fell heavily on to the seat, the blood dark and frightening, staining the pale leather. It made Sara aware of the helplessness of her position, with the Rolls incapacitated, and two injured people on her hands.

She drew back from the car and looked about her desperately, wondering if anyone else had heard the car horn. That had stopped now, leaving an ominous stillness, and she expelled her breath tearfully as she tried to think. Which was the nearest? Linden Court or the village? She looked down at her high heels despairingly. One way or another, she had to get help.

Of course, in the way of such things, there was no sign of another vehicle approaching, no reassuring gleam of headlights to offer any means of assistance. Harriet could be bleeding to death, and she was standing here cogitating. There was nothing else for it. She would have to run.

Before leaving, she felt compelled to check on the other driver, hesitating beside the car, her hands on the crumpled metal. The man saw her, turning his head towards her with evident impatience, clenching his hands tightly on the wheel.

'That was a bloody silly place to park a car!' he muttered, through gritted teeth, and a little of Sara's coldness left her.

'You were driving too fast,' she declared, realising anger might keep his spirits up far more than conciliation, and he blustered indignantly in spite of the pain he was probably suffering. He seemed to be pinned in his seat, the mess of metal beneath the steering wheel a hideous trap from which he would have to be extricated.

'Just get me out of here,' he begged, and a sense of urgency gripped her, sending her stumbling awkwardly across the grass in the general direction of Linden Court.

She took off her shoes after the first ankle-wrenching minutes, the damp grass infinitely soothing to her bruised feet. It enabled her to run faster, although her pace was uncertain until she could see the lights of the house.

The man striding through the belt of trees that bordered the parkland had no chance to avoid her breathless plunge. The first thing he was aware of was a slim, lissom form, that caught his body a glancing blow, before responding to the impact and collapsing weakly into the undergrowth.

For Sara's part, the identity of the man was of less importance than his actually being there. Someone else, another human being with whom to share her anxieties; she was already scrambling to her feet, when his hands came to assist her.

'In God's name, what is going on?'

Jude's harsh tones were so familiar, so *welcome*, that for a moment all Sara could do was collapse against him, warm and secure within the reluctant circle of his arms.

'Sara! Sara, for heaven's sake, what's happened?' he demanded after the briefest of pauses, and she forced herself upright, as she endeavoured to explain.

'The car——' she got out, panting as she did so.

'There—there's been an accident——'

'An accident! What kind of an accident?' Jude's hands shook her a little now. 'Sara, quickly! What happened? Is anyone hurt?' His voice lowered, and if Sara had been in any doubt that he had feelings for Harriet they were quickly dispersed by his hoarse intake of breath. 'Harriet!' he muttered. 'Has something happened to Harriet? Is she injured?'

Sara could only nod, and with an oath, Jude shook her once again. 'Where? Where is she? Have you sent for an ambulance?'

In stilted sentences, Sara managed to explain what had occurred, and Jude's reactions told her all she needed to know. Leaving her to make her own way up to the house, he sprinted away between the trees, and by the time Sara stumbled up on to the terrace, the sound of the ambulance's siren winding its way up from the cottage hospital was audible.

Rob took Sara home, after all, arriving some time later in Jude's dark red Mercedes. Sara was still in a state of shock, being served hot cups of strong sweet tea by a curiously subdued Venetia, who seemed to have shed her hostility along with her tears.

Not that Sara had much conversation with anyone. Jude had briefly outlined what had happened, before returning to the scene of the accident. Apparently he had heard the car's horn blowing, and this was why Sara had encountered him where she did. He had guessed something was wrong, but not the full extent of his own involvement. Sara had had to admire his coolness of purpose. In similar circumstances, she thought she might have run to the car first, to assure herself that Harriet was still alive and breathing. But Jude had immediately gone for professional assistance, realising at once that he himself could do nothing.

Both Rupert and Lord Hadley had accompanied Jude.

The party had quickly broken up in the wake of such news, and by the time Rob arrived to take Sara home, the drawing room looked bleak and deserted.

The journey back to Knight's Ferry was not one Sara wanted to repeat. By now, Harriet and the driver of the second vehicle had been taken away from the scene, but there were lights in the lane, and the police investigative team were involved with the calculations. Sara turned her eyes away from the mangled mess of metal and wondered with a pang when she would have to make a statement.

'Have—have you heard anything?' she ventured to Rob, who had always treated her with kindliness in the past, but he shook his head.

'Master Jude will let us know, as soon as he has any news,' he told her grimly, and Sara could only assume he blamed her for what had happened.

'Has—has Jude gone to the hospital with—Harriet?' she persisted, needing to know, and Rob nodded.

'Jude, and old Hadley,' he declared, squaring his shoulders. 'Only right, seeing as how he drove her to it.'

Sara blinked. 'He—he didn't drive her. I did,' she protested, but Rob only gave her a pitying glance.

'I'm not talking about the accident,' he exclaimed, giving an impatient sniff. 'Seems like you all got something to answer for, don't it? And Miss Ferrars is only trying to even the score.'

Sara decided she must have hit her head when she dived into the ditch. She was totally confused. Rob's words didn't make sense, at least not to her, and the throbbing pain of reaction was far worse than any migraine she had suffered. She just wanted to crawl into bed, and pull the covers over her head and forget everything that had happened this evening. But the selfishness of that wish made her despise herself utterly, guilty as she was of the most basic kind of deceit.

Janet was waiting for them on their return, her dour

features drawn into an expression of accusation: 'Ye're all right, I see,' she remarked, as Sara came into the hall, hugging her coat about her. 'Yon accident didnae send you to the hospital. But my poor mistress is in a bad way, so I hear.'

'You've heard! You've heard from Jude?'

Sara ignored the Scotswoman's scathing tongue in her eager quest for news, but Janet only snorted. 'Nae. We've heard nae more. Just what the laddie told us, afore Rob went to bring you home.'

'Give it a rest, Janet.' It was Rob who spoke then, his lined face showing a trace of compassion. 'You know perfectly well that Miss Shelley wasn't even in the car when it was hit.'

'Very convenient,' muttered Janet, turning away, but Sara refused to take offence. Janet was worried, they were all worried, and it was natural that she, as the innocent catalyst, should bear the brunt of the blame.

'I should go to bed, if I were you, lassie,' Rob suggested, gesturing towards the stairs. 'You look all in. There's nothing any of us can do tonight. You might as well get some sleep.'

'Oh, no.' Sara shook her head. She was tired, but she knew better than to think she could sleep before she knew exactly how serious Harriet's injuries were. She would have offered to go to the hospital with Jude, if she had been given the chance, but it had been obvious he did not want her with him. She doubted if he had wanted the Hadleys either, but they had not given him an opportunity to refuse. 'I'll wait,' she told Rob now. 'I want to be here when Jude phones. I—I'll go up and change this dress, though. It seems to be covered in mud.'

'Okay.' Rob glanced thoughtfully at his wife's departing back, and then added in an undertone: 'You won't take too much notice of anything Janet says just now, will you? She's upset. She doesn't mean anything.'

'That's all right, Rob.' Sara was too weary to care one

way or the other. 'I just hope we hear soon.'

'Master Jude will ring the minute he knows anything,' Rob assured her. 'He cares about her more than any of us, even if he does sometimes have a funny way of showing it.'

CHAPTER NINE

IT was the sound of the decanter that awakened her, the chink as the stopper was laid on the tray, and the steady pouring of the liquid into a glass. Sara opened her eyes with a start, blinking in the sudden illumination, and saw to her astonishment that Jude was standing by the cabinet.

Immediately she was aware of her state of undress. After removing the green dress, which she had rolled up in a ball and stuffed with some revulsion in the bottom of the closet, she had decided there was not much point in putting on more clothes. In consequence, she had pulled on the woolly white towelling bathrobe over her cream cotton pyjamas, and curled up in the armchair in the library, waiting for the phone call that never came.

Jude was aware of her awakening the minute she opened her eyes. His own eyes were heavy-lidded and bloodshot, and although he was still fully dressed, his appearance was somewhat dishevelled. There were stains on the sleeve of his velvet jacket—*blood?* she wondered, with a quiver of apprehension—and his thick hair was rumpled above the shadow on his jawline, where nature relentlessly showed no compassion. And as she looked at him, Jude raised the glass he had just filled to his lips, tilting his head back thirstily to reveal the column of his throat. His shirt neck was open, his tie discarded to appear half in and half out of his jacket pocket, and the immaculate appearance he had presented earlier was no more disturbing to Sara's emotions than his haggard fascination now.

Discomfited by his appraisal, Sara broke into hasty speech: 'You were going to phone! Did you phone? I—I mustn't have heard you. I must have slept——'

'I didn't phone,' said Jude flatly, examining the liquid left in the glass before putting it down, and Sara caught her breath.

'Is anything wrong? Has anything happened? Oh, God——' Her voice broke on a sob, and she thrust her bare feet to the floor: 'Is Harriet worse?'

'No, no.' Jude spoke almost impatiently, thrusting back his hair with weary fingers before viewing her with mild cynicism. 'But it's good to know you could sleep with a clear conscience. You'll need a clear head this morning when Sergeant Briggs comes to interview you.'

Sara got to her feet. 'I'm sorry if you think I've been careless. I didn't intend to go to sleep. But I remember waiting and waiting——' She paused, steeling herself against his mockery: 'What time is it?'

'Nearly six, I guess,' Jude replied laconically, moving to the windows to draw back the curtains and reveal a grey morning, and Sara gasped.

'Six!' she echoed. 'And you didn't phone! Oh, what must Janet have been thinking——'

'Don't worry about the Grahams,' Jude interrupted her shortly. 'The Hadleys called here on their way home from the hospital, about two o'clock. You were already asleep, so they didn't disturb you.'

'Oh!' Sara's cheeks burned. 'What must they have thought?'

'That you were tired, I guess,' retorted Jude dryly. 'Aren't you more interested in how Harriet is than what the Hadleys may have thought?'

'Oh—of course!' Sara wrapped her arms closely about herself. 'I'm sorry. I'm so stupid. How—how is Harriet? Has she regained consciousness?'

'A little over an hour ago,' Jude agreed, inclining his

head. 'I waited until she did, so that I could speak to her. But she was still a little dazed. She couldn't remember what had happened.'

'But how is she?' exclaimed Sara anxiously. 'The—the cut on her head—is that all that's wrong with her? I mean—I realise there may be concussion——'

'She has a fractured skull,' said Jude flatly, and Sara caught her breath. 'Just a hairline crack,' he continued matter-of-factly. 'So far as we know, there are no complications.'

'But the cut——'

'Head wounds always look worse than they are,' replied Jude. 'At least, that's what they tell me. Cuts bleed a lot, but it was the actual blow that did the damage. She must have cracked her head on the dashboard or the windscreen. They're not sure which. Either way, it was the impact that did it.'

'Yes.' Sara's palms covered her cheeks as she remembered the whole horrifying incident. 'I shouldn't have left the car in the lane. I should have closed the gate somehow——'

'Don't be silly!' Jude cut her off without compassion. 'It wasn't your fault. You might just as well say it was mine for not driving you both home.'

'No, but I should have closed the gate before I drove into the lane——'

'How could you? The Rolls would have been far more of a hazard jutting into the road. Be sensible, Sara, if you had left the car in that position, Harriet would most likely be dead now.'

Sara looked up at him. 'You—you think the accident might still have happened?'

'The way that young fool was driving, I'd say it was practically a certainty.'

'But how do you know?' Sara was hesitant.

'The force of the impact.' Jude shrugged. 'Sara, no one's blaming you, least of all Harriet.'

Sara swallowed convulsively. 'And—and she is going to be all right?'

'So they say. It's a little early to be absolutely sure, I suppose, but Harriet's a tough old bird. She'll survive.'

His words were curiously contradictory, coming from a man who the night before had been almost incoherent with anxiety. But they reminded Sara of her own feelings of the night before, and the indisputable proof of Jude's involvement with her aunt. They made her take an involuntary step backward, as if physically rejecting the brief sense of kinship they had shared when speaking of the accident.

'The other man,' Sara said now, her words coming quickly, as if to distract Jude's attention from that revealing gesture. 'Is—is he going to be all right? He—he seemed trapped.'

'He was. But fortunately he was wearing boots, those long cowboy boots some young men seem to favour. Still, I guess the leather saved his legs from getting badly lacerated. He had a cut or two, and a couple of broken bones, but he's not seriously injured.'

'Thank heavens!'

Sara was fervent, and Jude arched his dark brows. 'Why? Did you know him?'

'No. No, of course not.' Sara shook her head. 'Only—well, I'm glad no one was seriously hurt.'

Jude walked back to the cabinet and lifted his glass. 'He deserved to break his bloody neck,' he retorted grimly, swallowing the remainder of the Scotch. He replaced the glass on the tray and looked at her. 'He might have killed you, have you thought of that? You told me you'd got out to close the gate. If you'd been in the road . . .'

Sara shivered. 'Well, I wasn't. And he didn't. Honestly, I'm perfectly all right.'

'Are you?' Jude was regarding her strangely. 'No after-effects of the party?'

'The party?' Sara moved her shoulders bewilderedly. 'It seems such a long time ago.'

'Doesn't it?' Jude nodded, his eyes disturbingly intent.

'Harriet,' said Sara suddenly, almost using the name as a talisman, although against what she would not consider, 'will—I mean, when will she be coming home?'

'I don't know.' Jude made a dismissive gesture. 'Not today anyway. I expect you want to see her?'

'Of course I want to see her.' Sara spoke impatiently. 'I just wondered how—how long she might be in the hospital.'

Jude folded his arms across his broad chest. 'Really?'

'Yes.' Sara had the feeling that she should not have started this, but it had seemed an innocent enough question. 'Did—did the doctors give you any idea how long these things take?'

'Always supposing there are no complications?'

'Always supposing that, of course.'

'Then—one week, maybe two, depending how she responds.'

'Two weeks!' Sara was appalled.

'It may be necessary to employ a nurse after she gets home,' Jude remarked flatly. 'These things take time and attention.'

'I know.' Sara moved agitatedly, rubbing her elbows with the palms of her hands. 'I—I just can't help feeling resp——'

'What's the matter?' Jude interrupted her harshly. 'Doesn't the prospect of us being alone here appeal to you?'

Sara gasped. 'I—why—that has nothing to do with it. Be—besides, we're hardly alone, are we? Rob and Janet——'

'——have no brief to interfere in our affairs,' Jude finished for her. 'While Harriet's away I'm master here, or had you forgotten?'

Sara took an unwary backward step and came up against the desk. 'I don't think this is either the time or the place to be discussing such things,' she declared stiffly. 'You—you must be tired. I—I should go to bed, if I were you. I'll have Janet wake you if there are any developments.'

'Will you?'

To her dismay, Jude's tall frame successfully blocked her exit. Feet apart, his arms still folded across his chest, his slightly raffish appearance in no way detracting from his dark good looks, he was a formidable barrier, and her pulses raced in spite of herself. But the memory of Harriet, prostrate in a hospital bed, was sufficient to dispel any unwelcome emotion.

'I'd like to go to my room,' she said distantly, her linked fingers clasped tightly together. 'If you'd move out of my way . . .'

'You're going to leave me?' he mocked. 'You're going to abandon me to my lonely bed?'

Sara's face blazed with colour. 'That's not funny, Jude. Please—get out of my way. I want to go to my room.'

'It wasn't intended to be funny,' he remarked, taking absolutely no notice of her pleas to let her go. 'It's true.' His eyes darkened. 'My bed is lonely. Are you going to tell me you don't want to share it?'

Sara's jaw shook. 'You—you're disgusting, do you know that? I—I should have expected something like this from you. You have no conscience, do you?'

'Not a lot,' he admitted indifferently. 'I leave that to professed little virgins like you.'

Sara's chest heaved. 'You had to bring that up, didn't you?'

'Why not? It's relevant. It's why you're so damn scared to be alone with me!'

'That's not true.'

'What is true, then? That you don't feel anything when we're together? That when I touch you, you don't respond? Come off it, Sara, you know how it is between us. And just because Harriet has other plans for you, it doesn't mean we can't—precipitate your education.'

'You—you——'

Jude cast an exasperated look heavenward. 'Oh, can't we miss out the outraged maiden bit? I know, I'm a bastard—I've been told so many times. But——' his mouth softened sensually, 'you could change all that.' He took a measured step towards her. 'Doesn't that appeal to your virtuous nature? Taming the savage beast?'

'Nothing about you appeals to me!' she exclaimed, her hands gripping the desk at either side of her. 'I don't know how you can do this. With Harriet lying—possibly unconscious—in her hospital bed! Have you no shame?'

Jude drew a deep breath, and now the sensuality in his face fled, to be displaced by a scowling impatience. 'Look,' he said, taking another step towards her, 'I think it's time this façade was shattered. I don't know what Harriet's told you, but I can guess it was nothing complimentary. However, I think we've played around long enough——'

'Keep away from me!'

Sara thrust one shaking hand out in front of her, as if to ward him off, but Jude took no notice. 'Before you came here, I couldn't have cared less what happened to you. I didn't know you, and as far as I could see, you deserved everything you got.'

'I don't want to hear this.' Sara turned her head stiffly aside, but still he persisted.

'I mean—let's face it,' he said, 'you didn't think about Harriet until you were desperate. And then you came here, prepared to live on her charity, and accused me of being a parasite!'

'That's not true!' Sara's head spun round. 'I mean—I was wrong about you, I admit that, but I was not prepared to live on Harriet's charity. I wanted to get a job. I offered to get a job——'

'And have you got one?' His brows arched, and she lowered her eyes. 'Anyway,' he went on harshly, 'you're not a stranger any more. You're here, you're real, you've got an identity. And I can't go on pretending that what happens to you doesn't matter to me.'

Sara's nails dug into the wood of the desk as she straightened her spine. Then summoning all her small store of confidence, she looked up into his brooding face. 'Do you think I care what you think of me?' she demanded, choking back the sob that rose in her throat. 'Oh, all right, you can—make me do things for which I despise myself afterwards, but you're clever like that, you're experienced—you said so yourself. And—and you know I'd never betray you to Harriet. Not for your sake,' she hastened, 'for hers!' She shook her head. 'But as for you pretending you care about anyone but yourself, don't—don't make me laugh!'

She had some idea of charging past him then, of taking advantage of his sense of anger at her words to gain the comparative safety of the hall. But Jude was instantly aware of her intention, and his hand gripping her upper arm brought her uncomfortably close to his hard strength.

'You still don't understand, do you?' he snarled. 'You still persist in pursuing this ridiculous charade, for which I admit, I do share some responsibility——'

'Will you please let me go?'

Sara tried to freeze him with a glance, but his lean dark features were still absurdly disruptive to her chaotic state of mind. He was leaning towards her, his face drawn and intense, and her own weakened emotions were not aided by a blind surge of raw awareness. Even as he was, with his shirt pulled awry, blood smeared on his sleeve, and the growth of a night's beard shadowing his jawline, he stirred her senses as no other man had ever proved himself capable of doing, and she knew with a feeling of outrage his continued nearness was exerting an effect.

'Let me go,' she pleaded, refusing to give him the satisfaction of struggling with him, but those hard fingers gripping her arm only tightened their grasp.

'You're a silly little girl,' he told her harshly, his face only inches from hers. 'Do you really believe my living here is what *I* want?' He shook his head, his expression bitter. 'Harriet rejected me, Sara. She sent me away, when it suited her purpose to do so, and brought me back only to try and make James Hadley suffer!'

'*James* Hadley!' Sara caught her breath. 'Are—are you implying that—that Harriet had—had a—relationship with Lord Hadley?'

'They had an affair,' retorted Jude bleakly. 'Why don't you call it by its real name? Or is the term offensive to your priggish sense of morality?'

'I'm not priggish!' Sara was indignant. 'And—and why should I belive you? You could be telling me a pack of lies, knowing full well I could never ask Harriet such a thing.'

Jude expelled his breath impatiently. 'Why do you think she brought you here? When your father wrote——'

'My father never wrote to Harriet!' cried Sara contemptuously, tearing herself away. 'That's where you've made your mistake! It was Harriet who wrote to me, after—after she had heard of my father's death.'

Jude's jaw hardened, and for a moment his eyes were silver spears, impaling her at a glance. Then, with an almost defeated gesture, he lifted his shoulders, letting them fall with supreme inconsequence. 'Why am I doing this?' he asked, but the question was only rhetorical. 'You seem determined to take the line of least resistance. Maybe it's what /ou deserve. But I deserve something, too . . .' and before she could divine his attention, his hand had cupped her face, and his lips had covered hers.

She had no way of supporting herself except by reaching for him, and her fingers groped automatically for the lapels of his jacket. It was to be a momentary steadying, sufficient only to restore her sense of balance, but that involuntary reaction had not taken into account the insidious sensuality of his mouth. As she swayed closer to him, his lips pried hers apart, and the ensuing sweetness robbed her legs of all strength. She clutched at him then, and his arms slipped about her, while his other hand slid behind her head and loosened her carefully bound hair.

'Let me,' he breathed, in answer to her automatic

objection, 'let me, Sara. Don't drive me away.'

'We can't do this,' she choked, when he freed her mouth to seek the scented hollow of her shoulder, but her own bones betrayed her, rising to meet the caressing stroke of his tongue.

'Be quiet,' he ordered her softly, when his mouth returned to hers, and beneath its increasingly passionate onslaught, her protests were largely stifled. Her whole body seemed to be responding without any conscious volition, and her own fingers slid beneath his jacket to separate the buttons of his shirt.

His skin was chilled, but it warmed to her touch, tiny whorls of dark hair coiling themselves about her fingers. He shuddered when she touched him, but he did not draw back, and she knew a sudden awareness of her own instinctive reactions. She wanted to tear away the clothes between them, feel his muscled strength against her softness, and discover for herself the secrets of her own body, aroused by the thrusting maleness of his.

'Sara, Sara, Sara . . .' he groaned, pushing the folds of the towelling bathrobe off her shoulders, while his mouth played havoc with the pulse that palpitated wildly below her ear. 'Let's go to my room. We can be sure we won't be interrupted there . . .'

The warning lights that hitherto had been muted by the bemusing veil of emotion suddenly shone out bright and clear. Go to *his* room, Jude had said, but what room did he mean? His room or *Harriet's*? The significance of the distinction made all Sara's blood run to ice.

'*No!*' she gasped suffocatingly. 'No. Let me go! Let me go! You must let me go! I—I've got to get out of here—*now!*'

She had hardly had time to gather her robe about her when the knock sounded at the door, and after only a cursory hesitation it was opened. Janet stood in the aperture, her sharp eyes taking in every detail of what was happening, Sara was sure; and while to anyone else it must be obvious what had been going on, Janet's hostile disapproval focussed on Sara's state of distress.

'I'm sorry to interrupt, Master Jude,' she intoned, with grim eloquence, 'but I was wondering if ye'd be wanting your breakfast before or after ye went for your bath.'

Jude was recovering himself more slowly than on that occasion when Frank Barnes had interrupted them. Glancing surreptitiously at him, Sara saw, with an unwilling sense of compassion, that he did not look at all well, and the tiredness which had etched those lines about his mouth was now also evident in the hollowing sockets of his eyes. When he found her eyes upon him, however, his expression changed to one of cold loathing, and she retreated before his malignant gaze, with more than her own self-derision to keep her company. In that brief moment he had shifted the full weight of what had happened on to her shoulders, and worse than that, she knew her own culpability.

'I—er—don't bother about breakfast for me, Janet,' Jude said at length, pushing back his hair with a weary hand. 'I'll get my bath. I promised Harriet I'd be back at the hospital before ten, and all I seem to need is sleep.'

'Och, weel, you take care now, d'ye hear me?' Janet exclaimed, while Sara tried to inch her way towards the door. 'There was never no good in starving ye'self, and ye'd feel a might stronger with some porridge inside ye.'

Jude lifted a placatory hand. 'All right, all right. Just give me time to get a wash and a shave . . .'

'And Miss Shelley?'

Janet swung round on the girl, just as she thought she was going to make good her escape, and Sara wrapped her arms around her waist, almost protectively. 'Oh, you know me, Janet,' she stammered uncomfortably. 'Just—just a cup of coffee will do. Any time. It's not urgent.'

'Miss Shelley was just leaving,' Jude inserted harshly, and ignoring Janet's cluck of disapproval, he reached for the bottle of scotch again. 'Medicinal purposes,' he offered, as the housekeeper shook her head, and Sara slipped away silently, before anything more damning was said.

CHAPTER TEN

SARA had plenty of time to ponder the things Jude had told her. In the days that followed, when she was not at the hospital visiting Harriet, or parrying Rupert's attempts to further their association, she spent hours alone with her thoughts. Generally they were not productive. Indeed, she would rather not have had time to think at all. But two things stood out in her mind and refused to be dismissed—Harriet's previous relationship with Lord Hadley, and Sara's own continuing entanglement in her aunt's and Jude's affair.

It was impossible to resurrect those moments in the library without trying to find some meaning behind them. Yet Jude could only be using her to humiliate Harriet. What other motive could he have when he continued to live in Harriet's house, and behaved as if it was his unassailable right to do so? He did not love her, Sara. Their relationship was wholly physical; and she refused to consider what she might do if she ever conceived a deeper attachment. But it would not happen, it *could* not happen, and somehow she must ensure that circumstances did not conspire to allow it to happen.

She believed in those early days of Harriet's illness that it might not prove as difficult as she had first imagined. To begin with, Jude was seldom around. When he was not at his work or at the hospital, where he was obviously a welcome visitor, he kept very much out of her way, and they seldom if ever sat down to a meal together.

That Jude was angry with her she had no doubt. It was evident in the way he avoided her, and evident, too, in the hard malevolence of his gaze whenever they did chance to meet. He did not speak to her, unless she spoke to him first, and if she made some reference to Harriet, he obstinately refused to discuss the other woman. So far as he was concerned, any normal association between them was at an end, and Sara couldn't deny the feeling of desolation this frequently aroused in her. If only things had been different, she thought. If only she had met him at the Hadleys', as Lord Hadley's assistant—and not her aunt's lover!

Harriet herself made satisfactory progress. In a few days she was almost recovered from the shock of the accident, and although her body was weak, her mind was as alert as ever. She wanted to hear all about the accident, and about Sara's statement to Sergeant Briggs, and she had her own opinion to offer of the defendant's driving.

'You might have been killed, do you realise that!' she exclaimed, and Sara thought affectionately how typical it was of Harriet to think of someone else and not herself.

'I was in no danger,' she assured her aunt gently. 'It was just an unfortunate accident. You'll be happy to know that the young man, the other driver, is now out of hospital, so no one was seriously injured.'

'What about me?' Harriet's expression had undergone an acute change. 'How can you say that, when I'm still lying here as helpless as a kitten!'

'Oh, well—of course, you're still very weak,' Sara exclaimed hastily, 'but you'll be home soon, and the police sergeant said that the other driver was lucky to escape with his life.'

'Lucky!' Harriet snorted, and Sara tried to calm her down by patting her hand where it lay on the bedspread.

'Dear Harriet,' she said, 'I'm not excusing him. I'm only trying to make you see that it could have been so much worse.'

'I know. *You* could have been killed!' declared Harriet peevishly. 'And then—and then what—oh—yes, let's forget it, as you say. Obviously, you're still alive, and just as beautiful as ever.'

Harriet's words sparked off memories of what Jude had said, and Sara's smile was a little forced now. As if perceiving this, Harriet added: 'But you are looking a little tired, darling. Those lines around your eyes—I hope you're not still worrying about me.'

'No. No. That is——' Realising how ambiguous this sounded, Sara revised her words. 'I mean, we were all worried. But now that you're making such good progress——'

'It's not Jude, is it?' Harriet asked, with sudden perception, and Sara wondered if her expression was so revealing.

'No,' she denied now, plucking at the hem of the coverlet. 'I told you, we've been worried about you, that's all. Jude—well, Jude has been very upset, as you know.'

It was difficult to talk about Jude with the knowledge of Harriet's affair with Lord Hadley uppermost in her mind. Somehow it made it all so much worse and she wished she had not raised the subject.

Harriet, however, had no such misgivings. 'Yes,' she mused. 'Yes, Jude was quite amazingly disturbed, wasn't he? I must admit, it reassured me considerably.'

Sara bent her head, hoping the action would be construed as a silent acquiescence, and Harriet went on after a moment: 'He hasn't—how shall I put it?—tried to influence you in any way, since I've been in here, has he?'

'Influence me?' Sara was startled. 'How? In what way?'

Harriet sighed. 'Oh—well, against me, I suppose——'

'No!'

In spite of Sara's vehemence, Harriet was still concerned, and after considering her words she said: 'I shouldn't like to think that you might—believe—everything he tells you. I mean, I know Jude, I know how jealous he can be, and if he thought——'

'There's hardly been any conversation between us,' Sara interrupted her quickly. 'He—he's out of the house most of the time. I—I've hardly seen him.'

'That's good.'

Harriet looked a little more relaxed, and Sara wondered for a moment whether she had been a little hasty in imagining that her aunt did not suspect her relationship with Jude. From the tone of this conversation, one would think Harriet had some reason for asking these questions, and the thought suddenly struck her that perhaps Jude had deliberately set out to make mischief between them. Was it conceivable that he had lied to her? For the first time Sara wondered if the things he had told her were true.

It was unfortunate that Harriet chose that moment to misinterpret her silence. Unaware of the conflicting emotions playing across her face, Sara was totally unprepared for Harriet's next challenge, but her appalled expression was answer enough.

'I suppose he did find time to tell you about myself and James Hadley,' she remarked, almost as if it was of no consequence. 'I thought so. After what happened at the party, it was not inconceivable.' Her lips twisted. 'Come, come, Sara, surely you're not shocked? Don't you belong to the generation that condones such things?'

'I—I——' Sara was finding it incredibly difficult to think of anything to say. Why on earth should Harriet have jumped to this conclusion? What possible reason did she think Jude could have had to discuss Harriet's affairs with her?

'Don't look so flabbergasted, Sara.' Harriet's shoulders sagged a little wearily against the pillows now. 'Oh, I know what I did was wrong, but Lord knows, I've paid for it, one way and another.'

Sara was tempted to ask *how*, but she was glad she had kept silent when Harriet went on: 'You don't know what it's been like all these years, watching James's family grow up, knowing he would never let me be a part of it. He refused to marry me, you know. Even after Margaret was dead. He said it wouldn't be fair to Rupert and Venetia.' She shook her head, her eyes filling with tears. 'What did I care about Rupert and Venetia? Didn't I have some rights, too?'

Sara could see she was beginning to upset herself again, and she soothed Harriet's hand between both of hers, trying to reassure her. It was strange, she thought wryly, Harriet could arouse her sympathies almost without trying, just when she had thought herself immune.

After a moment her aunt recovered herself again, but she retained her grip on Sara's fingers as she looked up at her. 'You do understand, don't you, darling?' she asked appealingly. 'I was young, and foolish. I thought James intended to get a divorce or I would never . . .'

'Please.' Sara made a dismissing gesture. 'Let's not talk about it any more. It's nothing to do with me how—how you choose to live your life.'

'I knew you'd see it my way.' Harriet visibly relaxed. 'How could you not when I know you find Rupert just as attractive as I did his father!' She paused, giving Sara a moment to absorb this unexpected development, and then went on: 'Only you're luckier than I was. Rupert's not married. And when he came to see me this morning, he made it perfectly plain that he's interested in you.'

Sara straightened her spine. 'Rupert came to see you this morning?'

'Yes.' Harriet was matter-of-fact. 'He's been to see me a couple of times since the night of the party.' She smiled conspiratorially. 'I rather think he wanted to sound out my feelings about his association with you.'

'His association with me!' Sara knew she must sound rather stupid, but so far as she was aware, she and Rupert had had no association, at least, not yet.

'Don't pretend you're not aware of his interest in you,' Harriet asserted a trifle impatiently, as Sara continued to look blank. 'He tells me he's phoned you on several occasions since the party.'

'Well—yes. Yes, he has. But we haven't met.'

'I know that. He explained that you'd told him that

with me here in the hospital you didn't feel you could make any arrangements.'

'That's right.'

'Well, I want you to.'

'You want me to what?'

'Don't be obtuse, Sara. I want you to accept Rupert's invitation, next time he rings. There's no earthly need for you to worry about me. As you say, I'm on the mend. And I'll mend all the sooner if I know you're out enjoying yourself.'

Sara sat back in the chair beside Harriet's bed. 'You *want* me to go out with Rupert?'

'Of course.'

'But he's practically engaged!'

'Who told you that?'

'I can't remember now. Venetia, I think.'

'She would.' Harriet snorted. 'Elizabeth Carthew is her best friend. She and her father have done everything in their power to push Rupert to propose.'

'And you want to throw a spanner in the works,' murmured Sara thoughtfully, unconsciously paraphrasing what Venetia had said, and Harriet's expression convulsed.

'Who told you that?' she demanded. 'Oh, don't tell me, I can guess. Jude has been talking to you, hasn't he? I wonder what other lies he's concocted for your benefit!'

'It wasn't Jude,' Sara heard herself defending him, even though she guessed Harriet would not believe her. 'It—it was just the impression I gained, that's all. And—and if I do go out with Rupert, won't I be doing just that?'

Harriet's brows formed a suspicious line. 'Your friendship with Rupert is your affair, yours and Rupert's. It has nothing to do with anyone else. Not Venetia, or her father, or Jude. And especially not Elizabeth Carthew!'

Sara knew herself backed into a corner, but still she looked for escape routes. 'Nevertheless, I wouldn't like to upset anyone——'

'Oh, don't be silly. The only person you'll upset if you persist in this is me! Good heavens, girl, you're far more suitable to fit the role of lady of the manor than that insipid Carthew creature!'

'Now wait a minute . . .' Sara had to protest then. 'Harriet, I know he was sweet to me at the party, but there's no question——'

'Why not?'

'Why not?' Sara looked aghast. 'Why, because it's too soon to even consider such a thing! I hardly know him. And he doesn't know me——'

'He likes you. He likes you very much.'

'How do you know that?'

'He told me.'

'You discussed me with him?'

Harriet looked smug. 'I didn't have to. He couldn't wait to tell me what he thought about you.'

Sara shook her head. 'I—I think you're exaggerating——'

'No, I'm not.' Harriet leant forward to squeeze Sara's hand now. 'Isn't it exciting?' She smiled, and the girl wondered why she could not respond. 'Just imagine—my niece could be the next Lady Hadley! Have you thought of that?'

Sara thought about it all the way home, and contrary to Harriet's expectations, she found the whole idea rather unpalatable. It wasn't that she didn't like Rupert. On the contrary, she had found him quite a pleasant young man. But for Harriet to be considering marriage, at a time like this, left her with the unpleasant suspicion that Jude's warnings to her had not been as self-indulgent as she had thought. Yet why was Harriet doing this? What on earth could she get out of it? And after the way James Hadley had treated her, it hardly made sense!

Rupert rang that evening, and when Janet called her to the phone, Sara went with an uneasy mind. Right now, the last thing she wanted was to get involved with anybody, but with Harriet's words ringing in her ears she felt obliged to be friendly.

It was easier than she had expected. Ruper. was *so* understanding. When she cried off from his invitation to have dinner with him later in the week, he immediately suggested walking over the following evening, and Sara had no objections to his joining her for a drink.

In fact, Sara found Rupert rather a pleasant young man, away from his home and his father's influence. It was true his main interests seemed to be horses and other sporting activities, and his conversation was liberally dispersed with frivolous comments, but Sara welcomed his inconsequential chatter after the strained atmosphere that prevailed at Knight's Ferry. What did it matter if he was brash and a little immature? Just because he and Jude were much of an age it did not mean she had to make comparisons between them. Rupert was much less complicated, and she ignored Janet's scowl of disapproval when she asked if they might have some coffee.

After that evening she accepted Rupert's invitation to have dinner with him in Buford two days later, and when she told Harriet, as she was obliged to do, her aunt was suitably gratified.

'What did I tell you?' she exclaimed, giving a smug smile, and Sara wished she felt more enthusiastic, and less like a manipulated doll. Somehow, no matter how much she might enjoy Rupert's company when she was with him, she couldn't forget why she was doing this, and she determined that once Harriet was home from the hospital she would make her decisions for the right reasons. Indeed, it might be easier for all of them if she returned to London, as Jude had once suggested, and a letter from Laura seemed a significant omen.

The other girl, however, was feeling rather low. An attack of influenza had left her without much energy, and unable to return to her job at the hospital until she was completely recovered, she was finding her days long and lonely. Reading between the lines, Sara guessed Laura would have welcomed an invitation to spend a few days in the country, and had Harriet been at home and in good health she would certainly have broached the subject. But she couldn't invite anyone here while Harriet was in hospital, particularly not when she and Jude were barely on speaking terms. The alternative was for her to visit Laura, but how could she leave Harriet until she was home?

It was a problem, and it stayed with her throughout the next couple of days. Even her outing with Rupert did not help to ease her troubled thoughts, and she was afraid she was rather short with him when he suggested coming in for a drink after bringing her home.

'Not tonight, Rupert,' she exclaimed, extricating herself from his arms after permitting a salutory goodnight kiss. 'I'm tired,' she added, using that hackneyed old cliché, and his mouth turned down sulkily as he had to let her go.

'I'll ring you,' he said, without confirming the suggestion he had offered earlier in the evening that he might show her round his home at the weekend, and Sara was glad to agree. If Harriet was put out that she was not to see Rupert any more this week, it was just too bad, and at least Rupert would hardly be likely to complain about his own lack of success.

Locking the outer door behind her, Sara pushed her coat into the cloakroom and climbed the stairs. The house was in darkness, apart from one lamp which illuminated the landing, and she guessed Rob and Janet had gone to bed, knowing she had her own key. It reminded her of that other occasion when she had thought herself the only person awake; but Jude had been there in the library, and their forbidden relationship had begun.

She shivered, and as she did so a door opened below her, and a shaft of light appeared. She paused, half prepared to meet Janet's growing hostility, and found Jude looking up at her from the entrance to the library. He was in his shirt sleeves, and his eyes looked shadowed, as if he had been working, but the glass in his hand seemed to deny this. He looked dark and brooding, and dangerously angry, and her fingers flexed and unflexed against the polished wood of the banister.

'Come down here,' he commanded, gesturing to the library behind him. 'I want to talk to you.'

'Well, I don't want to talk to you,' declared Sara, keeping the tremor out of her voice with difficulty. She couldn't imagine what he might have to say to her, but whatever it was it could wait until morning. 'I'm tired,' she said, using the excuse she had given Rupert. 'If you'll excuse me . . .'

'I'm tired, too,' he retorted, taking two steps across the hall. 'However, I intend having this out with you tonight, whatever state of health you may be in.'

Sara quivered. 'Whatever you have to say to me, I'd rather you said it in the morning, when you're—less— less——'

'——intoxicated?' he demanded harshly.

'*Angry*,' Sara replied. 'As—as you haven't opened your mouth to me for the better part of a week, I can't see that a few hours more or less will make any difference.'

'Can't you?' He had reached the foot of the stairs now, and was looking up at her with cold malevolence. 'Do you come down, or do I come up? It's all the same to me.'

Sara hesitated. She didn't know what to do. She had no wish to have a conversation with him in this mood, and she couldn't quite believe that he would do as he threatened and follow her upstairs. After all, he could hardly follow her into her bedroom—*could he*?

She licked her lips. 'If it's to do with Harriet, I saw her earlier——'

'It's nothing to do with Harriet. At least——' he shrugged, 'not in the way you mean.'

'Then it can wait till morning,' exclaimed Sara tightly. 'As—as a matter of fact, I wanted to talk to you. About a letter I had from a girl friend. I—I suggest we meet for breakfast——'

'Now,' stated Jude uncompromisingly, and with a jerky

expellation of her breath Sara shook her head.

'No,' she said, keeping her voice firm and deliberately turned and walked up the rest of the stairs.

Any fears she had had that he might come charging upstairs after her were proved groundless. Although she was sure he watched her as she mounted the last few stairs and walked across the landing, he made no move to follow her, and she breathed a sigh of relief when her door closed behind her. She had made it. It was only a pity there was no key to lock her door, although perhaps that would have been rather silly.

Stripping off her evening dress, she padded into the bathroom, sluicing her face thoroughly under the tap and cleaning her teeth with rare fervency. But the small activity helped to keep her mind blank, and she refused to consider what revelations she might have to face in the morning. She glanced at her reflection before re-entering the bedroom, her expression twisting wryly as she recognised that look of nervous agitation. Good heavens, she thought, what was wrong with her that she couldn't have a conversation with Jude without becoming emotionally disturbed? He was a man, that was all, just a man, a man moreover who seemed to think he had only to speak for any woman to jump to his bidding.

Shaking her hair loose from the clasp that had held it at her nape, she came back into the bedroom, only to stop short at the sight that met her startled gaze. Jude was lounging on the turned-down bed, still fully dressed, but obviously determined to make her eat her words.

Immediately her hands flew to her breasts, and her face suffused with colour at the realisation that her panties were scarcely a covering. Made of silk and lace, they were a concession to decency, no more, and she had removed her tights earlier, before going to the bathroom.

'G—get out!' She almost screamed the words in her horror, but Jude made no move to obey.

'I have seen your breasts before, you know,' he

remarked, with cold emphasis. 'Now, do stop behaving in that girlish fashion, and listen to what I have to say.'

Sara would listen to nothing. She was humiliated and outraged, and the sight of him lounging on her bed filled her with anger and indignation. 'Will you get—get out of here?' she choked, clinging to her attitude, and Jude's mouth compressed impatiently as he viewed her helpless frustration.

'So much fuss,' he exclaimed in a bored voice. 'For heaven's sake, Sara, grow up!'

'Grow up?' Sara nearly choked on the words. 'You—you force your way into my bedroom——'

'Correction, I knocked, and when you didn't answer I opened the door,' Jude inserted, but she ignored him.

'You force your way in here—you—you lie on my bed, and—and then have the nerve to tell me to—grow up!'

'Oh——'

He said a word Sara would not care to repeat, and then swung his legs to the floor. But her hopes that he might be going to leave her were unfounded. Instead he lifted the cotton wrapper that was lying on the foot of the bed and advanced towards her with it in his hands.

'Keep—keep away!'

Sara could not take her hands from her body to hold him from her, but she kicked out with her legs and caught him a glancing blow on his shins. She was sure it hurt her toes more than it hurt his leg, but the simple incident seemed to incite the anger which had briefly been smouldering. With a smothered oath he flung the wrapper aside and reached for her, hauling her close against his hard body, and in the ensuing struggle Sara lost all hope of retaining her dignity.

'Crazy little fool!' he snapped, as she endeavoured to escape him. 'Why the hell can't you behave like any normal female?'

'By fawning all over you, I suppose,' she gasped, as he forced her hands from her body and imprisoned them at her sides, and Jude's eyes darkened.

'I said I intended to talk to you,' he retorted. 'I invited you to join me downstairs. You chose the venue, not me. Now you've got to take the consequences.'

'What consequences?' she demanded, quivering as his eyes moved over her, and with a groan, he shook his head.

'I think you know,' he muttered huskily, and gripping her waist he pulled her to him.

She should have fought him then, but she couldn't. When his mouth covered hers, she was shocked into awareness, and the most obvious awareness was an increasing desire to submit. She had never been naked in a man's embrace before, and the fact that the man was Jude robbed her of all resistance. Close in his arms, with the roughness of his belt chafing her midriff, she was helpless in the grip of emotions that refused to be controlled. After the way she had treated Rupert she should have been equally prepared to repulse the overtures of another man, but with Jude it was never like that. With his hand warm against her spine, promoting an urgent intimacy between them, she could feel herself yielding, and the taut demin of his pants could not disguise his growing arousal.

'You know what I want,' he said against her mouth, his warm breath sweet and wine-scented. 'You want it, too. I can feel it. And God help me, Sara, I don't want to wait——'

'You—you must.' Sara shifted anxiously against him, as commonsense and her conscience fought to gain precedence. 'Jude, you can't do this. You mustn't do this. Can't—can't we talk in the morning?'

'Like hell!' he muttered, his hands sliding up her spine, his thumbs deliberately brushing the hard peaks of her breasts. Sara trembled as her body responded, but still her eyes protested, and with a sound of impatience Jude took her face between his palms.

'All right,' he said huskily, bending his head to rub his

tongue against her lips, 'tell me to go and I'll go. But don't pretend it's what you want, because I won't believe you.'

Sara moved her head helplessly from side to side. It would have been easier, she thought, if he had forced her. Then she would have had a reason to resist. Now, with his grey eyes on her, his thin dark face waiting for her reply, she found herself incapable of sending him away.

'Oh—Jude,' she breathed, winding her arms around his neck, and with a groan of satisfaction he gathered her up into his arms.

The sheets of the bed had never felt softer or more sensuous than they did against her bare skin. Or perhaps it was Jude, on the bed beside her, his eager hands and exploring fingers taking possession of her in a way she had never imagined.

She had expected he would turn the lamp off, but he didn't, and her heart thumped at a palpitating pace when his hands went to release the buckle of his belt. She turned her eyes aside from what he was obviously doing, and for an awful moment cold reason returned to chill her flesh.

'Harriet——' she objected, as he came down on the bed beside her, sleek and brown-skinned and supple as a cat, but he only silenced her with a deep and searching kiss.

'To hell with Harriet,' he muttered, pulling her beneath him, and the delight of feeling his muscled body close to hers stilled any further protest she might have wished to make.

'The light,' she exclaimed anxiously, when he shifted to one side to run warm possessive fingers down over her flat stomach, and his expression grew meltingly indulgent.

'I want to look at you,' he told her softly, following the path of his fingers with his lips. 'I want to possess you. I want to touch you—and taste you—and make you want me as much as I want you.'

Sara found she was responding in spite of the lingering

...ions that were urging her to fight him. Her body ...med to have a will of its own, and it instinctively knew what he wanted her to do. Against her own volition, it seemed, she was twisting and turning and arching against him, and when a wave of sweetness brought a sudden weakness to her legs, she trembled on the brink of real experience.

'Now,' he breathed, sliding over her to find her parted lips with his own, and her hands sought and convulsively gripped the hair at his nape.

'Now!' she cried wildly, hardly aware of what she was doing and his mouth stifled the sob that rose in her throat as a stabbing pain ripped through her . . .

It was the pain that she remembered when Jude lay still beside her. With her eyes fixed on the curtains, moving softly in the draught from the window, and the lamplight shifting in patterns on the ceiling, she could almost have pretended that nothing had happened—if it hadn't been for the pain!

Of course, she had been incredibly naïve. She hadn't considered—she hadn't realised—how *physical* it would be. To contemplate what Jude had done, to re-live those moments when he had invaded her body, brought a shivering revulsion, and she couldn't imagine how she could have willed such a thing to happen feeling the way she did right now. She wished he would go. She wished he would get up from her bed and let her go into the bathroom and wash away her guilt and her pain. She felt she would never be able to face Harriet again, and for what? she asked herself bitterly.

When Jude moved she stiffened, holding herself completely still as he levered himself up beside her. She even closed her eyes, praying he would think she was asleep and leave her, but a probing finger across her lips showed how futile that was.

'Do you hate me?' he asked huskily, as her eyes flickered open, revealing their dry wounded depths to his gaze.

'Did no one ever warn you how it was?'

'It's not the sort of thing one discusses with anyone else, is it?' she declared tightly. 'But—but as it's over, perhaps you'd go now.'

Jude's mouth twisted. 'Sara, I didn't want to hurt you, but believe me, it'll never happen again——'

'I'll make sure it doesn't!' With a shiver of apprehension Sara struggled up on to her elbows, but when she would have swung her legs off the bed, one of his legs prevented her.

'Wait,' he said huskily, imprisoning her beneath him, but Sara only panicked and raked his shoulder with her nails.

'For heaven's sake,' she cried. 'What do you want from me! You—you've seduced me! Isn't that enough?'

'Not nearly,' he told her roughly, his expression gentle as she still tried to get free of him. 'Sara, Sara—it can be so much better. Let me show you how making love should be.'

'Now?' Sara was horrified.

'Now,' he agreed softly, pushing the moist hair back from her forehead, but Sara was appalled.

'You can't——'

'Why can't I?'

'I—I don't want you to touch me again.'

'You don't want me to hurt you again,' he amended dryly. 'Believe it or not, you hurt me, too.'

'I did?' Sara was briefly diverted, but then she shook her head. 'Just go away, please. I want to be alone.'

Jude's mouth tightened. 'You know, I'm tempted to take you at your word.'

'I wish you would.' Sara turned her face away from him.

'Do you?'

Jude was silent for so long, she was compelled to turn and look at him, and her stomach wobbled at the unwilling awareness that she still found him disturbingly attractive. As he lay unashamedly beside her, his lean muscled body open to her gaze, she felt the unwelcome stirrings of feelings she had hoped extinguished by his brutal assault. But they were still there, and she averted her eyes in case he should become aware of it, too.

'Sara!' he muttered impatiently, misinterpreting that suddenly veiled glance. 'Oh, for God's sake!' and with a backward movement he got off the bed, leaving her looking after him in troubled bewilderment.

'Where are you going?' she asked, foolishly she realised, but the words were out before she could stop them.

'To get good and drunk,' retorted Jude, reaching for his trousers, and hardly aware of what she was inviting, Sara struggled on to her knees.

'Do—do you hate me?' she stammered now, needing to know. 'I mean—I was—*I am*—in a state of panic, I know that. But—but I have—have to accept—some blame——'

'Blame!' Jude glared at her, swearing as he struggled to get one leg into his jeans. 'You know something? You're not real!'

Sara quivered. 'Jude, listen to me——'

'Why should I? You wouldn't listen to me!'

'Jude, please——'

'Please what?'

He halted abruptly, looking down at her, his fingers on the point of zipping up his pants. Hardly knowing what she was doing, Sara stretched out her hand and stayed his, and his choked protest was wrung from him: '*Sara!*'

'Don't—don't go,' she said unsteadily, giving in to emotions too strong to be ignored. 'Stay with me——'

'If I stay with you——'

'I know,' she silenced him huskily. 'I must be out of my mind!'

'You're driving me out of mine,' Jude retorted grimly, but when he joined her on the bed, it was a very desirable kind of insanity . . .

CHAPTER ELEVEN

HE was gone when Sara awakened. The rattle of teacups disturbed her heavy eyes, but when she lifted her lids it was to see Janet standing over her with a tray. Immediately one hand groped across the place beside her, but to her relief she was alone and Janet was none the wiser.

'It's ay eleven o'clock,' she declared disapprovingly, as Sara wrapped the sheet about her. 'It's no my place to tell ye when ye should be up, but I'm thinking ye'll not be wanting to miss Miss Russell's call.'

Sara was blank and confused, torn by guilt and self-recrimination, and totally incapable of comprehending what Janet was going on about. 'Miss Russell's call?' she echoed faintly. 'Laura—called here?'

'She telephoned,' agreed Janet shortly. 'Soon after nine. But Master Jude wouldn't let me disturb you then.'

'He wouldn't?' Sara's face flamed with revealing colour. 'He—he took the call?'

'Noo.' Janet shook her head. 'He just said to ask the lassie to ring back later. And I'm telling ye, she said she'd ring again after eleven.'

'I see.' Sara moistened her dry lips. 'And—and where is Jude?'

'Where would the laddie be but at his work?' Janet demanded dourly. 'Not all of us can lie abed till nigh on noon. I'll be leaving the tray.'

'Oh—oh, yes. Thank you.' Sara shifted across the bed so that the housekeeper could put it down beside her. 'I—I'm sorry I overslept, I—don't know why I'm so tired.'

'Do ye no?' Janet's brows beetled. 'And what time were ye to bed last night? Gallivanting till all hours with that

157

young man. I don't know what Miss Ferrars is thinking of, that I don't. Can't she see Lord Hadley will never stand for it?'

'I—I wasn't out until all hours,' Sara contradicted her quietly. 'I—I was home quite early, actually. About half past ten.'

'Were ye now?' Janet's gaze grew speculative, and Sara realised that by defending the length of time she had spent with Rupert she was leaving herself open to other questions.

'Yes,' she said hastily now. 'I—I was tired.' Then she looked down at the tray. 'This—this really is kind of you, you know. It—wasn't necessary.'

'Master Jude's orders,' retorted Janet stiffly, making for the door. 'See you eat it,' and with an unexpected softening of her features she went out of the room, leaving Sara with the distinct impression that for once Janet was not angry with her.

On the tray was a silver rack of toast, some curls of butter and marmalade, and a delicious pot of coffee. But first there was a glass of fresh orange juice, and as she sipped it Sara felt the unwilling stirring of recollection. She didn't want to think about what had happened the night before. She didn't want to remember her own shameless behaviour. But now that her mind was alert again, the memories were irresistible, and in spite of her good intentions, waves of weakness swept over her. Dear God, she thought, as the aching sweetness of fulfilment made all her senses tingle, and she might never have known what making love was all about! If she and Jude had parted in anger . . . She sighed. Yet perhaps it might have been better if she had remained in ignorance, she amended silently. For, having shared the experience with Jude, how could she ever contemplate sharing it with anybody else?

A trembling languor took possession of her, and unable to deny the urgent demands her body was making, she lay back voluptuously against the pillows. If she closed her eyes she could almost feel Jude's possessive hands upon her, and the persuasive abrasion of his mouth as he hungrily drank from its sweetness. His ardour had known no bounds, and her body had opened to him. She had wanted him then, she had wanted all of him, and that powerful surge within her had satisfied her every need. There had been no pain, only pleasure, no revulsion, only an aching desire to please him as he was pleasing her, and then the ultimate satisfaction, as they both reached the heights together . . .

Afterwards, she had been bemused and sleepy, content to fall asleep against him, with his male scent all about her. Even when he awakened her again, in the cool dark hours before dawn, she had responded without hesitation, eager to experience that forbidden ecstasy again. And it was only now, in the cold light of day, that guilt and self-contempt were surfacing, to make what had happened a thing of shame and torment.

Banishing the treacherous memories from her thoughts, she hastily poured herself a reviving cup of coffee, and then got determinedly out of bed. But her legs were weak and she swayed before steadying herself, her wanton nakedness another lash to flay her conscience. Yet, human nature being what it is, she could not prevent an involuntary glance at her reflection. Somehow she had expected what had happened to show, but apart from a slight bruising here and there, her body looked as wholesome as it had ever done. Only she knew it was not, she thought tremulously, and despised herself for the reaction she still could not control.

She was in the shower when Janet came tapping at the bathroom door, and she remembered belatedly why the housekeeper had wakened her. Laura had rung. How could she have forgotten? Was she so selfish, so absorbed with her own feelings, that not even the knowledge of her friend's call could penetrate the egotistical barrier of her thoughts.

'Yon lassie's on the phone again,' Janet called, as Sara turned off the water. 'Will I tell her ye're coming to take the call?'

'Yes. Yes, please, Janet.' Sara hastily wrapped the fluffy pink bath sheet about her and opened the bathroom door. 'Tell her I won't be a minute. I'm sorry for the delay. I— I thought I had more time.'

She doubted Janet believed her, but she went away, and Sara quickly brushed her hair and put on the towelling bathrobe to go downstairs. She didn't bother dressing. There wasn't the time. And besides, there was only Janet to witness her *déshabille*.

She wondered as she descended the stairs why on earth Laura should be ringing. After all, she had only had her letter two days ago. She hoped nothing serious had happened.

Curling up on the velvet armchair in the hall, she lifted the receiver. 'Laura? Laura, how lovely to hear from you. I'm so sorry I wasn't up sooner to take your call.'

'Oh, don't worry.' To her relief, Laura sounded much the same as usual. 'It's my nursing training, I suppose. I'm always awake soon after seven.'

'Yes.' Sara wished she could think of a suitable response, but she couldn't. Laura would probably be horrified if she told her the truth, and pressing her lips together, she said instead: 'So—how are you? How's the 'flu? I was going to write to you today.'

'As a matter of fact, that's why I'm ringing.' Laura took a deep breath. 'Look, Sara, is there any chance of your coming up here for a few days?'

Sara swallowed convulsively. 'I—I don't know——'

'I wish you would.' Laura sounded pretty fed up now. 'You don't know what it's like here. The flat's so empty, and since Tony went on night duty . . .'

'Tony's gone on nights?' Sara sighed. Tony was Laura's next door neighbour, and she guessed her friend would miss his cheerful company.

'That's right,' Laura agreed now. 'It would just happen when I was off. It never rains, isn't that what they say?'

Sara hesitated. 'I'd love to come up and see you, Laura, you know I would, but actually, we've had something of a—well, an accident down here. Harriet's in hospital——'

'In hospital?'

'——with a fractured skull,' Sara finished, and then briefly outlined what had happened, without mentioning Jude's part in the affair. Laura did not even know of Jude's existence, and somehow Sara did not think she would approve if she did.

Laura was concerned. 'I'm so sorry. You must stay there, of course. Please give her my best wishes the next time that you see her.'

'I will.' Sara felt even worse. Oh, God, she thought, if only she could escape to London until Harriet came back to Knight's Ferry.

The sound of a door slamming brought her round with a start to find the reason for her bitter recriminations strolling indolently across the hall towards her. In close-fitting corded slacks and a wine-coloured silk shirt, his jacket looped lazily over one shoulder, he looked dark and attractive, and irritatingly pleased with himself, and Sara jerked round sharply, denying her leaping senses.

A hand snaking over her shoulder and down inside the hastily drawn neckline of her bathrobe brought a look of horrified indignation to her face, but his mouth only curved indulgently as her breast swelled to his touch. 'Get rid of them, whoever it is,' he ordered huskily, and his mouth against her neck was almost her undoing.

'Who are you talking to?' Laura had heard the muffled words, and Sara hastily put her fingers over the mouthpiece.

'Do you mind? she exclaimed, sliding off the velvet armchair and moving away from him. 'I'm speaking to Laura.'

'I know it,' he said indifferently. 'Janet told me.' He
lounged into the armchair she had just vacated and
crossed one booted ankle over his knee. Then, with lazily
caressing eyes, he asked: 'Did you sleep well?'

Sara couldn't look at him, and turning her back, she
leaned against the wall. 'Look, someone's come in,' she
said, speaking to Laura again. 'I think I'd better call you
back.'

'Okay.' Laura sounded puzzled, but resigned. 'He sounds
male. Is it the boy-friend?'

Sara glanced round at Jude, then she turned back to
the phone. 'No,' she said distinctly. 'No, he's not my boy-
friend. He's my aunt's.'

It was as well she was replacing the receiver when
Jude's hand came down on hers, otherwise she would have
dropped it. 'You little bitch!' he grated, and she quailed
before the furious glitter of his eyes. 'You can't still believe
that trash, can you? After last night? Oh, *God*!' his lips
twisted contemptuously. 'You do believe it, don't you?
Lord Almighty, I could wring your little neck!'

He released her wrist so suddenly, Sara almost
stumbled, and she had to grasp the table to support herself. 'I—I don't know what you mean,' she cried, her
mind refusing to expand any further, and with a grunted
oath he grabbed her arm again and dragged her after
him into Harriet's sitting room.

The small desk where Harriet usually answered her letters was bare at present, but Jude seemed uncaring of the
fact that its drawers were private. With a cold suppressed
violence that chilled Sara to the bone, he wrenched out
the drawers one by one, spilling them and their contents
over the carpet. He was evidently looking for something,
though for what, Sara couldn't imagine, and she gulped
in apprehension when he suddenly gave an angry cry of
triumph.

The paper he thrust at her was old and mellowed, but
as with all such documents, its contents were still intact.

Briefly, it was a birth certificate, Jude's birth certificate, signifying that on the seventeenth of January 1951, Harriet Elizabeth Ferrars had given birth to a son.

Sara lifted her eyes to Jude's in some confusion. 'But—but this——'

'I think its authenticity is unmistakable, don't you?' he demanded bitterly, and she quivered.

'But—but this means——'

'——that Harriet is my mother. I know. Do you doubt it? Can you think of any other reason why I should feel responsible for her?'

Sara shook her head. 'But I thought——'

'I know what you thought,' he retorted coldly.

'It was a reasonable mistake.'

'Was it?'

'You know it was.' Sara looked down at the birth certificate again. 'But—but your father's name—it's missing.'

'I told you I was a bastard,' he declared flatly. 'So I am—Harriet's bastard. That's why you hadn't to know the truth.'

Sara was bewildered. 'But why? Why not? I—I'm not shocked or anything.' She lifted her shoulders in a helpless gesture. '*You* should have told me!'

Jude's mouth twisted. 'I thought the truth would have dawned on you by now. I'd forgotten what consummate deceivers women can be. Even after—well, even though you let me—take you last night, you still believed I was Harriet's lover!'

She looked at him helplessly, seeing the pain and contempt in his expression.

'You—you know why I let you—make love to me last night,' she said at last. 'I couldn't help myself. I—I love you.'

'You—*love me*!' His laughter was crueller than anything she had ever heard. 'Oh, now I've heard everything.' He used his boot to kick the strewn papers on the hearth.

'You don't love anybody but yourself, Sara. You'd better save that line for Rupert. He's the one Harriet's chosen for your future husband!'

He left her then, striding out of the room without a backward glance, leaving her to stare dry-eyed at the mess he had left behind him. She hoped if Janet came in she would not imagine she had done this, but as she was indirectly responsible, it was up to her to clear it up.

She tried not to look at the letters as she gathered them all together. Harriet's correspondence was nothing to do with her, and she had no doubt her aunt would be furious if she found out what Jude had done. And she would certainly find out that Sara now knew Jude's identity. Sara herself intended to tell her.

One letter, however, did attract her unwilling attention. It had an Indian stamp on it, and when she reluctantly examined the envelope, she recognised her father's handwriting. Puzzled, she turned the letter over, and as she did so something else Jude had said came back to her. He had told her her father had written to Harriet, but she had denied it. Certainly she had known of no such letter, and Harriet had never admitted to being in correspondence with Charles Shelley.

It was not something she would normally do, but these were hardly normal circumstances, she reflected dryly, as she drew the letter out of the envelope. She had to know why her father had written to Harriet without telling her anything about it.

There was a photograph of herself inside the letter, and it spilled out on to the floor as she unfolded the sheet. It had been taken in India, only a few weeks before her father died, and showed her wearing the sari, beside the swimming pool at the hotel in Calcutta.

Even more puzzled, she looked at her father's handwriting, and as she read what he had written a sense of pain and indignation gripped her. Harriet should have told her, she thought in growing horror, she should not have kept this from her. Oh, how could she have kept this news to herself when it put an entirely different reflection on her father's death!

The letter was simple enough. It was a plea for help: not for himself, but for his daughter. Charles Shelley had written that he had recently discovered he had cancer, and that he had only a short time to live. *The drugs!* thought Sara aghast, and read on. Her father had obviously contacted Harriet in the hope that she might give Sara a home after he was dead. He wrote that he had persuaded his doctor to keep the truth from Sara, and although there had been a post-mortem, the true circumstances of his illness had never been revealed.

That was something she had to think about, but more cruelly, Harriet had left her in ignorance. She had let her go on thinking her father had taken his own life because he couldn't face his debts, when in fact he had been trying to save her from the inevitable cost of his own illness. Harriet had even pretended she had only learned of Charles Shelley's death through the newspapers, when in all probability he had arranged that she should be informed.

It took her fully an hour to restore the desk to rights, and she was closing the last drawer when Janet appeared in the doorway. Right on cue, thought Sara bitterly, in no mood to cross swords with her, and faced the older woman in silent defiance.

'Are you all right?' The Scotswoman eyed the girl's revealing appearance with unexpected compassion. 'Ye havenae been crying, have ye? The young master went storming out of here like a thundercloud, an' now ye're obviously upset.'

Sara bent her head. 'I'm all right, Janet. I must be picking up a cold, that's all. I—I'll go and get dressed. If you'll excuse me——'

'Your lunch——'

'Oh, I'm afraid I'm not very hungry.' Sara forced a

faint smile of apology.

'Wouldn't ye know it!' Janet put her hands on her hips. 'And himself not wanting the guid food I've prepared either.'

Sara pressed her hands together. 'I'm sorry.'

'Are ye?' Janet pursed her lips. 'An' what's been going on here, that's what I'd like to know? What has young Jude been telling ye? It cannae 'a been anythin' guid.'

Sara sighed. 'I'd really rather not talk about it.'

'Would ye nae?' Janet squared her shoulders. 'Away wi' ye, I can guess. I warned Miss Ferrars he'd never stand for it, but no, she wouldnae listen.'

Sara hesitated, curious in spite of herself. 'You—warned Harriet?'

'Aye, I did.' Janet sniffed. 'Denying her own flesh and blood! Is that the behaviour of a respectable woman?'

Sara expelled her breath tremulously. 'But why did she do it? Surely—surely people must suspect——'

'Och, it was nae a secret till you came.' She snorted. 'How could it be? When herself brought the laddie here to spite his lordship!'

Sara was growing more and more confused. 'Lord Hadley?' she asked faintly, and Janet nodded.

' 'Twas a cruel thing to do to both of them, I said it at the time, but a woman scorned is still a powerful enemy, and Miss Ferrars doesnae forget a grudge.'

Sara moistened her lips. It was becoming obvious Janet thought she knew more than she did, and rather than betray her ignorance Sara improvised a little.

'I—I suppose Lord Hadley resented Harriet having—having her son living with her,' she probed, and Janet, intent upon her story did not notice the tremor in her voice.

'Och, he was furious at first,' she agreed. 'And with guid reason, I suppose. It wasn't as if he hadnae paid for his mistake. Yon laddie had the best education money could buy, and his lordship himself approved of the couple who took the charge of him when he was a babby.'

Sara quivered. 'You mean—you mean—Jude is Lord Hadley's son?' she breathed incredulously, and Janet turned to her with accusing eyes.

'He didnae tell ye?'

'Not that, no.' Sara shook her head.

'Och, weel——' Janet shrugged her shoulders philosophically. 'Ye deserve to know. Seeing as ye know the rest.'

Sara sought a chair and sat down with rather a bump. 'I'm beginning to understand now.'

'Aye.' Janet hesitated a moment, as if regretting her sudden burst of confidence, but then evidently her affection for Jude overcame her misgivings. 'Ah, weel, it's all water under the bridge now.'

Sara looked up at her. 'Won't you tell me when Jude came to Knight's Ferry? You said—it was a cruel thing to do, bringing Jude here. Why?'

Janet sighed. 'Lord Hadley and Miss Ferrars—weel, when she was a lassie, she had some notion of marrying his lordship, but it wasnae realised. He was promised to his cousin Margaret, and he married her.'

Sara nodded. 'Jude—Jude tried to tell me something of this,' she murmured, remembering their conversation in the library. Only she had been too stubborn to listen to him, and he had lost his temper . . .

'Aye, I guessed he would.' Janet folded her hands. 'It's no a pretty story. My mistress must have regretted her recklessness many times over, but by then it was too late.'

'So what happened?'

Janet considered her words before continuing: 'To begin with there were nae children to the marriage. Don't ask me why. Sometimes it happens that way. Weel, his lordship came courting my mistress again, and she, fool that she was, let him have his way with her.'

Sara knew a momentary amusement at the old-fashioned words, but then the graver aspects of the situation weighed down on her again.

'Ye'll hae guessed, she became pregnant, and ye can imagine what manner of scandal that would hae caused. His lordship arranged for her to go away, to a little village in Scotland, where naebody knew her, and she could hae her baby in peace and comfort. That was my village.'

'I see.'

'Of course, he had to promise her all manner of things to make her do his bidding. Maybe he had some mind to put his wife away and take another. But then it was discovered that Lady Hadley was expecting a babby, too, and my puir mistress was out in the cold.'

Sara could feel sympathy then for the young Harriet, alone and unmarried with a baby on the way. Things were different in those days. Unmarried mothers were social pariahs, and the whole situation took on a new aspect.

'Weel, after the laddie was born, Lord Hadley arranged for him to be brought up by a respectable couple in Sussex, and young Jude attended the same boarding school as his half-brother.'

So that was why Jude and Rupert knew one another so well, thought Sara, as the pieces of the jigsaw began to fall into place. Their familiarity stemmed from their schooldays. It also explained why she had never heard of Jude, and why he had never accompanied her aunt on any of her visits to Sara's school. But how strange. To visit her cousin's daughter, but never her own son!

'Ye'll know his lordship's wife died when young Venetia was born,' Janet went on more reluctantly now, and when Sara nodded: 'It was then that my mistress's bitterness was born. Och, I told her it was madness to care after all these years, but she did—and who can say she didn't deserve some consideration?'

'She—expected Lord Hadley to marry her?'

Janet nodded dourly. 'It nearly killed her when he told her he'd never do it. He couldnae. He knew that if he married my mistress, she'd expect him to adopt Jude legally. An' how could he do that, and deprive his son of his birthright?'

'Oh!' Sara understood it all now. 'So—so Harriet brought Jude here to live with her, knowing how Lord Hadley would feel.'

'Aye, as I said, it was a cruel trick to play. Particularly on Jude.'

'I believe it.' Sara was aghast. 'But——' She looked up again. 'He does seem to care for her.'

'Och, that's right, he does.' Janet sniffed again. 'He's that kind o' mon. He may resent the mess she's made of his life, but he'd no hurt her.'

'The mess?'

'Aye. He'd taken his final exams at the university, ye see. He was going to study law. Miss Ferrars persuaded him to give that up, and brought him here, to work for his own father.'

'And—and what did Lord Hadley do? He gave him a job.'

'Och, have ye nae seen the two o' them together? Jude and his lordship, I mean. Sure, the mon thinks the sun shines out of him, and puir Rupert suffers in the comparison.'

'You're saying that—Lord Hadley loves Jude?'

'Aye, that I am.'

'And do his children know?'

'Rupert and Venetia?' Janet shrugged. 'I suspect Rupert has guessed. Venetia, no.'

'Oh, now I see——'

'——why Miss Ferrars gets so upset over Jude's friendship with his sister? Och, she has no need to worry. Jude's no interested in his own sister. His interest lies in another direction, I'm thinking.'

Sara, seeing the way Janet was looking at her, felt the familiar tide of embarrassment sweeping over her. 'Oh, no,' she said, shaking her head vigorously. 'Not—not after what's happened. I don't think he'll—ever—forgive me.'

Janet frowned. 'It's a bonny mess, I'll say that.'

'Yes.' Sara rose rather unsteadily to her feet.

'Ye care about him, don't ye?' Janet's eyes were intent. 'Miss Ferrars was more perceptive than I thought. Och, why ever did she conceive such a plan!'

Sara blinked back her tears, unable at that moment to either care or comprehend what plan Janet was talking about now. Her head was aching with the weight of all she had learned this morning, and she had no clear idea of what her own actions should be.

CHAPTER TWELVE

'How could you, Harriet!'

It was later the same day, and Sara was standing beside her aunt's bed in the hospital. After taking some aspirin she had put on her clothes and asked Rob if he would drive her into Buford. She wouldn't have dared to drive Jude's car anyway, and the Rolls-Royce was still in the garage being repaired, but Rob and Janet owned a small Austin, and it was this that had brought her to town.

'Darling, please sit down and stop glowering at me,' Harriet declared now, waving to the chair behind Sara. 'Can't we sit and discuss this like civilised people, without you attracting the Ward Sister's attention?'

Sara hesitated, but then, giving in, she slumped down into the chair, gazing at Harriet with wide accusing eyes. 'Very well,' she said, 'let's discuss it. But first of all, will you tell me why you lied about my father?'

Harriet shifted her pillows into a more comfortable position and then gave the girl facing her a cool appraising look. 'I?' she said icily. 'I did not lie about your father, Sara. So far as I remember, the circumstances of his death were never discussed.'

'We discussed him dying. We discussed the funeral arrangements——'

'Yes. And you told me that a post-mortem had been conducted.'

'It was.' Sara took a deep breath. 'They—they told me he had died from an overdose.'

'So he did.'

'Yes. But they omitted to tell me he'd had cancer!'

Harriet's mouth thinned. 'I never knew you were a sneak, Sara. What else did you find while you were routing through my desk?'

'I didn't—rout through your desk. Jude—Jude pulled the drawers out when he was looking for his birth certificate, and I—I put them back again.'

'I see.' Harriet regarded her without liking. 'Well, what was I supposed to do? Announce to you on your arrival that your father had been chronically ill? That he had taken his own live to save himself more pain?'

'It wasn't like that.' Sara was horrified. 'I know—I *knew* my father. You don't understand how things were. Medication was so expensive——'

'And he was a compulsive gambler!' declared Harriet brutally. 'You're defending a man who gambled on your own future.'

Sara was pale. 'He thought he knew you. He thought you might care.'

'And I did,' retorted Harriet shortly. 'I wrote to you. I offered you a home. What more could I have done?'

Faced with that implacable fact, Sara was helpless, and Harriet went on: 'Just because Jude's been filling your head with his own grievances it doesn't give you the right to come here and criticise me. All right, perhaps I should have told you your father was terminally ill. But what good would it have done? Would it have made you feel any better? Do you feel better knowing the truth?'

Sara opened her mouth to speak, and then closed it

again. Once again Harriet had chosen exactly the right attack. Did she feel any better? Could she honestly say that knowing her father had been dying and not told her made her feel less bitter? In all honesty, she had to admit that it did not, and Harriet pressed her advantage.

'You see,' she said triumphantly. 'You know that I'm right. You were beginning to get over it, and some day, who knows, I might have shown you that letter for myself.'

Sara was silent, and Harriet leaned forward to touch her sleeve. 'Have you been so unhappy with me, honestly?' she asked, her tone gentle now, and with a feeling of frustration Sara did not draw away.

'So,' Harriet relaxed against her pillows again, content at having won that particular round, 'let's forget all about it. And Jude, too. I'll speak to him myself later.'

Sara lifted heavy eyes. 'You should have told me,' she persisted. 'That Jude was your son, I mean. I thought—I thought——'

'I chose to keep that affair to myself,' Harriet interrupted her evenly. 'After all, we hardly knew one another. And,' she paused, for effect, Sara suspected, 'I'm not proud of that incident in my life.'

'Then why did you force Jude to come here?' exclaimed Sara. 'Why didn't you leave him alone? He was happy——'

'Oh, he's been pouring out his heart to you, hasn't he?'

'It wasn't Jude, it was Janet,' retorted Sara recklessly. 'She told me—everything.'

Harriet snorted impatiently. 'Oh, dear! I was afraid of that. She always was absurdly fond of the boy. She looked after me while I was expecting him, you know. Then, afterwards, she accompanied me back to England.' She laughed, rather wryly. 'She would have had me keep him, you know. Perhaps it would have been better if I had. Perhaps if James had seen him as a baby, as a small boy, growing up, he would have found him irresistible. He certainly seems besotted with him now.'

Sara shook her head. 'Why did you do it?'

'Do what? Bring him back to live with me? Didn't Janet tell you that as well?' She shrugged. 'I wanted to make James suffer. I wanted to make him squirm every time he looked at Jude. It was an appropriate choice of name, don't you think? Jude—Judas! I insisted on that small consideration.'

Sara sighed. 'But why did Lord Hadley employ him? Surely he didn't have to.'

'Ah . . .' Harriet touched her nose with her finger in a conspiratorial gesture. 'That was quite a brainwave of mine. You see, I knew James was looking for an assistant, and I mentioned that I knew of a young man who might suit the position. When he saw Jude, he knew who he was, of course. The resemblance is unmistakable, at least it is to us. And—well, Jude got the job. I don't think James could have refused, once he had seen him.'

'And Jude knew——'

'Not then.' Harriet looked a little discomfited by this question. 'Later. I told him—later. He didn't let me down.'

Sara was appalled. 'That—that was a foul trick to play!'

'Why?' Harriet held up her head. 'He owed it to me. He owes me a lot.'

Sara bent her head. It seemed as though the picture she had had of Harriet had crumbled, just as that earlier impression had crumbled when first she came to Knight's Ferry. She didn't feel she knew her any more. She wasn't even sure she wanted to.

Lifting her head again, she took a deep breath. 'I—I'm thinking of going away for a while, Harriet,' she said bravely. 'To—to London. Laura—that's that nursing friend of mine—she's been ill, and I'm going to go and stay with her.'

Harriet's lips drew in, but she merely lifted her shoulders in a gesture of acceptance. 'Very well,' she said. 'When will you be back?'

'I don't know.' Sara hesitated. 'I don't know whether I will be coming back.'

'What!' Harriet was aroused now. 'What do you mean? Of course you're coming back. It's the Hunt Ball in three weeks, and I know Rupert is planning——'

'I'm not interested in what Rupert's planning to do,' said Sara steadily. 'Oh, I've begun to realise what you had in mind. At first I didn't, but now I'm beginning to see. You——you want me to marry Rupert, don't you? To make up for all the humiliation you suffered——'

'Is that so outrageous?' demanded Harriet harshly, but Sara could only shake her head.

'It——it wouldn't work, Harriet. It couldn't ever work. I——I don't love Rupert——'

'Love!' Harriet was scathing. 'What is love? I loved his father, and look what that gained me!'

'Nevertheless,' Sara insisted, 'I don't want to marry Rupert. I'm not interested in his——his money and his title——'

'You'd rather live in a suburban semi, and look after a swarm of squealing brats, I suppose!'

'If I loved their father, of course,' Sara responded fiercely.

'What a waste!' Harriet's lips twisted. 'With your looks——'

'Is that when you conceived this idea, Harriet?' Sara asked bitterly. 'When you saw my picture? I wonder what you'd have done if I'd been fat and homely.'

'Who knows?' Harriet refused to be drawn, her features cold and distant, and Sara rose to her feet.

'I'm going now, Harriet,' she said, and when the other woman didn't answer, she impulsively bent and kissed her cheek. 'Thank you,' she said. 'I don't know how I'm going to repay you. But I'll send you some money, as soon as I have a job——'

'I don't want your money.' Harriet was scornful. Then: 'Have you told Jude you're leaving?' She paused, and finally added: 'I think you should.'

'No.' Sara shook her head again. 'I don't think he and I have anything more to say to one another. Give him—give him my—my best wishes. In case I don't see him before I leave.'

It was after midnight when Sara's train pulled into Paddington Station. She had missed the earlier express, which would have got her into London soon after ten o'clock, and the later train was infinitely slower and more noisy. In consequence, it was nearly half past one when her taxi stopped outside Laura's flat in Benchley Street, and she hoped rather apprehensively that her friend was at home.

She had not returned to Knight's Ferry.

After leaving the hospital, she had wandered round for a while, uncertain what she should do. But the idea of returning to Knight's Ferry and possibly seeing Jude did not bear thinking about, particularly now that he knew how she felt about him. She didn't want his scorn or his amusement, and the thought that he might pity her had sent her hurrying to the phone.

Janet had been disapproving of her plans, but Sara could not have left without reassuring her. 'I—I don't know when I'll be back, Janet,' she said, avoiding a straight answer, and the Scotswoman had had to accept that she would not change her mind.

'You watch what you're doing, miss,' the taxi driver said now, as she paid him his fare. 'Not safe to be about alone at this time of the night. You sure your friend's expecting you?'

'Oh, I'm sure.' Sara was touched by his concern. 'I'll be all right. And—thank you.'

She thought he waited while she descended the steps to Laura's basement entrance, but she hoped he would not hang about and hear her hammering at the door. He might even begin to wonder whether she was entirely to be trusted, and the last thing she needed was a policeman checking her story.

It was dark in the well of the steps and she knew a moment's misgiving as she went down them. Tramps had been known to make their beds in sheltered basement entrances, and even a policeman would be preferable to one of them.

In consequence, her heart nearly leapt out of her breast when something moved in the shadow, and cold biting fingers dug into her shoulder. 'Relax, it's me!' Jude's harsh tones stifled the scream that rose in her throat, and she turned toward him incredulously, blind to everything except his voice.

'Jude!' she breathed, her fingers running disbelievingly over the soft leather of his jacket, and then: 'Oh, *Jude*!' as weakness flooded her whole system.

'Where the hell have you been?' he demanded unsteadily, both his hands sliding over the curve of her neck and shoulder. 'I've been waiting here for hours! I was beginning to think something had happened to you.'

'I—I missed the early train at Swindon, and the one I got stopped at every station,' she explained huskily. 'But—oh! what are *you* doing here? Did—did Harriet send you?'

Jude drew in his breath and she could feel the stiffening muscles beneath her fingers. 'No,' he muttered roughly, 'nobody sent me. Now, do you have a key, or do we stand here all night?'

Sara swallowed convulsively. 'Is—isn't Laura at home?'

'If you mean the girl who lives here, sure she's at home,' agreed Jude flatly. 'But she didn't know me from Adam, and she said she knew nothing about you coming to stay with her. I think she thought I was stringing her a line, to find out if she was alone in the place, and she certainly wouldn't let me in to wait for you on that shaky pretext.'

Sara felt her lips curving upward in spite of herself. 'Poor Laura,' she murmured, with a husky chuckle, and

Jude's fingers suddenly dug into her neck.

'What about me?' he exclaimed. 'I've been waiting for you since nine o'clock. Believe me, you owe me for the bad time you've given me!'

Sara quivered. 'I don't understand——'

'No. And I don't intend to conduct explanations on the doorstep,' Jude retorted shortly. 'Ring the bell or knock at the door, or do whatever is necessary to gain attention. I'm frozen!'

'Your car——'

'—is parked quarter of a mile away,' he finished for her. He gestured upward toward the street. 'There's no place to park around here, and I couldn't risk missing you and having your friend tell me you didn't want to speak to me.'

Sara caught her breath. 'I wouldn't have done that.'

'Wouldn't you?' Jude's voice had deepened. 'I wouldn't have blamed you if you had. I was pretty brutal to you this morning, wasn't I? But you made me so bloody mad——'

'Ssh!'

Sara lifted her fingers to his lips, but instead of allowing them to rest there, Jude turned her palm against his mouth, and she felt the moist probing of his tongue. 'Dear God, Sara,' he groaned, 'I've been nearly out of my mind——' and that searching caress was transferred to her mouth.

He was cold, she could feel it. With only the thin silk of his shirt between her and his hard body, the chilling dampness of his flesh was unmistakable, and she hastily drew back.

'You'll get pneumonia!' she choked, when her mouth was free, and then turned quickly as a light illuminated the dark area. Laura had turned on the lamp in the entry, and her faltering voice came to them in the sudden stillness.

'Sara? Sara, is that you?'

'Yes!' Sara pulled herself away from Jude's embrace

and put her mouth close to the still-closed door. 'Laura, open the door. It's chilly out here.'

'Are—are you alone?'

Laura's voice was still uncertain, and Sara sighed. 'No,' she said, 'Jude's with me. You know, the man who called earlier. Can we come in?'

Laura hesitated a moment longer, and then to her relief Sara heard the key turning and the bolt being drawn. The door opened to reveal her friend, pale and anxious in her woolly dressing gown, and Sara didn't hesitate before giving the other girl a hug.

'Hello, love,' she said. 'How are you? I'm so sorry to spring this upon you, but—well, it's a long story.'

Laura's eyes had moved to Jude who had entered the flat behind Sara, and was now closing the door behind him. She gave him a rather uncertain smile, and then returned her attention to Sara.

'What's going on?' she exclaimed, leading the way into the small living room. 'I thought you said you couldn't get away, Sara.' She shook her head. 'I'm afraid I didn't believe—your friend—when he said you were on your way here.'

'That's understandable.' Jude had positioned himself just inside the door, his hands pushed deep into his jacket pockets. 'I guess I must look quite a disreputable character. I'm afraid I didn't stop to shave before I left.'

Sara glanced at him quickly, but to her the dark shadow on his jawline only added to his attraction. The look they exchanged turned all her bones to water, and she could hardly concentrate on what Laura was saying as the other girl made her explanations.

'I mean, I didn't know who he was,' she was saying, switching on the electric fire. 'So far as I knew your aunt had no relatives. You never told me she had a son, Sara.'

Sara sighed. 'I—I didn't know.' She gave Jude an appealing look. 'Harriet didn't tell me.'

'It's a complicated affair,' he inserted flatly. He glanced

round. 'By the way, you don't have any Scotch, do you? Just to warm us up a little.'

'Only sherry, I'm afraid.' Laura gave an apologetic grimace. 'Will that do?'

'Thanks,' Jude nodded, and while Laura went to get the sherry from the kitchen, Sara went close to him again.

'Are you very cold?' she asked, pulling one of his hands from his pocket and chafing it between both hers.

'Nothing that you couldn't cure,' he retorted softly. 'Look, I have to talk to you. Is there any chance of us being alone together?'

Sara's pulses raced. 'There's only one bedroom. I—I share it with Laura.'

'Not tonight,' he said firmly, his eyes dark and intense, and Sara trembled.

'We—we can't,' she breathed. 'Not—not here——'

'I know that,' he said, impatiently, taking both her hands behind his back. 'But I want to spend the night with you, even if we have to spend it in armchairs!'

Sara's hands slid over his hips. 'Oh, Jude——'

'Don't do that, for God's sake,' he groaned, reluctantly propelling her away from him, and as he did so, Laura reappeared.

'Here we—oh! I'm sorry——'

'It's all right, Laura. Come in.' Sara turned to her at once, and the other girl handed her two glasses of sherry. 'Hmm, this is lovely,' she added, after giving one to Jude. 'An improvement on the cooking variety you used to have when I was here.'

Her words eased the awkwardness of the situation, and Laura glanced behind her. 'Look, I'll leave you two alone,' she offered. 'You obviously have a lot to—to talk about.'

'Oh, Laura——'

'No, really, I mean it.' Laura smiled. 'Mr Ferrars can stay the night if he wants to. If he doesn't mind using the sofa.'

'Thanks, Laura.'

Jude smiled, and for a moment Laura was mesmerised by his dark fascination. Then, pulling herself together, she squeezed Sara's arm and hurried out of the room, before either of them noticed her foolishness.

Alone at last, Jude put down his glass of sherry, and flung himself full length on the sofa. 'God, I've had it,' he muttered, running his fingers over his eyes, and Sara hastily disposed of her glass before kneeling down beside him.

'Are you all right?' she exclaimed, turning his face towards her, and he uttered a tired, but satisfied, sigh.

'Now I am,' he agreed huskily. 'If you forgive me.'

'Me? Forgive you?' she echoed faintly. 'I should ask you to forgive me. I shouldn't have been so quick to jump to conclusions.'

'Why not?' Jude grimaced. 'It was what Harriet intended. Or at least, she didn't want you to look in my direction when she was pointing you in another.'

'Rupert,' said Sara softly.

'Rupert,' he agreed.

'She was wasting her time.'

'Was she?' His head was resting on a cushion, his eyes dark and insistent turned towards her.

'You know she was,' replied Sara huskily.

'I know you always hated me for touching you.'

'I felt so guilty, didn't I?' Sara protested, her fingers moving over his jawline. 'When I thought you——'

'I know,' Jude overrode her roughly. 'God, there were times when I hated Harriet!'

'You could have told me,' Sara persisted, her hands finding the loose knot of his tie and pulling it free.

'What, when I suspected you might be like Harriet?' He closed his eyes for a moment. 'You know, I believed her when she told me you found Rupert attractive.' He opened his eyes again as Sara's widened in indignation. 'She said I shouldn't get any ideas about you. You wouldn't look at a poor estate agent when the estate owner was ripe for the bait.'

Sara gasped. 'She said that!'

'Something of the sort.' Jude shifted on to his side. 'Did you mean what you said this morning?'

Sara found she couldn't voice her feelings. She was too choked up. Instead she said: 'When did she say it? *Why* did she say it?'

'Why do you think?' Jude's hand circled the nape of her neck and caressed the soft skin. 'You know, she was right about one thing: you are beautiful.'

'Jude!' Sara shivered under his hands. 'You—you only answered half my question.'

'Mmm? Oh, yes. *When?*' He sighed. 'Several times, I guess. How about the night of the Hadleys' dinner party?'

Sara blinked. 'I heard you arguing that night. But I thought it was because you didn't want to go.'

'I didn't.' His thumb probed her lips, running the pad across her teeth. 'Why would I want to be a witness to your growing involvement with Rupert——'

'My *assumed* involvement.'

'Okay.' His mouth softened indulgently. 'Your assumed involvement. As it happened, I had to stand by and watch that idiot Hedgecomb undressing you with his eyes.'

'Was he doing that?'

Sara was appalled, but Jude's expression grew wry. 'You'd better believe it,' he said. 'So I decided it was time I did something about it.'

Sara frowned. 'But you went off with Venetia—Oh!' She broke off abruptly. 'Poor Venetia! She's crazy about you, you know.'

'Not any more.' Jude was phlegmatic. 'I told her the truth. That was what Harriet was so het up about.'

'Oh—oh, I see.' Sara remembered Venetia's tearful face with sudden comprehension. She also remembered how nice the other girl had been to her later. At least Venetia was no longer her enemy.

'We're wasting time,' Jude said now, drawing her face towards him and rubbing his lips against hers. 'Mmm, Sara, *Sara*—how am I going to sleep with you without loving you? Do you really think Laura would mind?'

Sara was breathing very fast, but with trembling fingers she pushed him to arm's length. 'We—we could get a room,' she ventured, and his lips curved into a lazy smile.

'Oh, Miss Shelley, what are you saying!' he teased, his eyes dancing, and the hot colour betrayed her once again.

'I—I only thought——'

'I know what you thought,' he declared, sobering. His mouth took on a sensual twist. 'And believe me, I'd like nothing better. But if I'm going to convince your friends that my intentions are honourable, I guess I shouldn't start by taking you to a hotel.'

'Honourable!' Sara sat back on her heels, hardly daring to believe what she was hearing, and Jude sat up and swung his legs to the floor.

'What did you think?' he demanded, taking both her unresisting hands in his and pressing them together. His eyes darkened. 'Is it such a shock to you?'

Sara nodded her head helplessly. 'Well, yes—*no*! I mean, I never dreamed——'

'What did you never dream?'

Sara bent her head. 'You—you don't have to do this, you know. Just—just because last night we——'

'Don't you want to marry me?' Jude's voice was harsh suddenly, and she looked up at him in wide-eyed confusion.

'I—I——'

'I thought you loved me!' he muttered, his hands gripping hers so tightly now, she could feel all the blood draining out of them.

'I—I did, *I do*!' she protested fiercely. 'But—but you never said——'

'Oh, God! That *I* loved *you*?' Jude made a sound of anguish. 'Dear heaven, I thought that was obvious. Didn't

I tell you so that morning in the library?'

'Wh—what morning?' Sara was tremulous.

'The morning after Harriet's accident,' exclaimed Jude impatiently. 'The morning I told you about her affair with—with my father.'

'Well, you were right about my father writing to her,' murmured Sara evasively. 'He—he had cancer. Did you know?'

'She told me,' admitted Jude flatly. 'Sara——'

Sara leaned towards him. 'You—you said you—you cared what happened to me——'

'And didn't that mean anything to you?'

'Well, yes, but I thought you were only trying to—to hurt Harriet——'

'Oh, *God*! What that woman has to answer for!' Jude's arms slid round her, and he lifted her bodily on to his knees. 'Hell,' he buried his face in the silky softness of her hair, 'why did you think I was so angry with you afterwards? I—I assumed——'

'—that Harriet had been right about me?'

'Yes.' He lifted his head, and his eyes were only inches from hers. 'Until last night.'

Sara quivered. 'Why did you change your mind?'

Jude shook his head. 'I didn't. At least not at first. I'm ashamed to say I eavesdropped on your goodnights with Rupert.' He grimaced. 'The things you and Harriet have made me do!' He shook his head. 'Anyway, I'd had a few drinks during the course of the evening, and when you came in and went straight upstairs, I guess I lost my head.'

'I'm glad you did.' Sara wound her arms around his neck.

'So am I,' he muttered fervently. 'Although I have to admit I've had some pretty bad moments today—*yesterday*.'

'Why?'

'Why?' He cast a brief look heavenward. 'After you

practically accused me of raping you!'

'That—that was when I was silly——'

'And afterwards?'

'Mmm.' Sara lifted her shoulders in voluptuous reminiscence. 'You know how it was.'

'*I* know how it was,' he agreed unsteadily. 'You know I love you, don't you? And I've learned not to use that word lightly.'

'Jude . . .' She drew his mouth to hers and caressed it urgently with her own. 'Oh, darling, I'm so glad you came after me.'

'Believe it or not, it was Janet who suggested it,' he admitted ruefully. 'I didn't know what to do. When I got home and discovered what had happened, I half believed I was to blame——'

'Oh, Jude——'

'—but Janet seemed to think you were more upset over what Harriet had done.'

'I was.' Sara was fervent. 'I told her so this afternoon.'

'Yes,' Jude nodded. 'I rang the hospital and spoke to her before I left. She didn't actually give me her blessing, but she sounded—resigned.'

Sara nodded her head. 'She did advise me to tell you what I planned to do.'

'Did she?' Jude looked impressed. 'Well, knowing how I felt about you, I guess that was pretty magnanimous of her.'

'She knows?'

'She knows,' Jude confirmed dryly. 'Why do you think she got my father to give that party? When she first brought you to Knight's Ferry, she thought she could take her time about introducing Rupert to you and getting him interested. But she's not stupid. She could see the way things were going between us and she was afraid I might spill the beans before she could make any headway.'

'But if she said I wouldn't look at you——'

'My weakness, I'm afraid,' he said wryly. 'I believed what she said, because I couldn't believe you might choose me and not Rupert.'

'Jude!' Sara gazed at him reproachfully.

'I know.' He gave her a rueful smile. 'But it's true. I can't give you the kind of life Rupert could give you. I mean, I have a little money of my own, but compared to him——'

'I'm not interested in him or his money,' Sara declared vehemently. 'I don't care where we live or what we do, so long as we're together. After living with my father all those years, I'm used to trying to make ends meet.'

'Well, it won't be as bad as that,' remarked Jude whimsically. 'My—my father has told me that when I want to get married, he'll give me a house on the estate. I'm entitled to it,' he added dryly. 'All the estate workers are.'

Sara sighed. 'Will—will she mind very much, do you think? Us living so close.'

Jude smiled. 'You know, I suspect she'll get over it sooner than you think. She's not really so bad. My father did deceive her, after all.'

Sara cradled his face between her palms. 'You're very forgiving.'

'I can afford to be. I've got what I want,' he replied steadily. 'And now I suggest I move to another chair, and let you have the couch.'

'No!' Sara was fervent. 'Don't—don't leave me! We can share the sofa—see?' She scrambled off his knee and stretched herself against the back of the sofa. 'There's plenty of room for both of us. Jude—I want to feel your arms around me.'

He looked a little strained, but he acquiesced, turning off the lamp before stretching out beside her, so that her back was against his chest. 'And if your friend comes in and finds us?' he asked, as she drew his arms around her, and Sara sighed.

'We're not doing anything wrong,' she protested, nestling closer against him, unaware that Jude had closed his eyes against the unknowing temptation of her slim body.

'Will your friend be going to work in the morning?' he asked, before her steady breathing told him she was asleep, and Sara shook her head.

'No. Laura's had 'flu and at present she's recuperating. The hospital won't let her go back to work until she's really fit.'

'She's a nurse?' Jude sounded reflective.

'Hmm. A Ward Sister.' Sara was sleepy. 'Why?'

'Well, I just thought she might like to come and stay at Knight's Ferry while we're on our honeymoon,' Jude replied, with forced detachment. 'After all, Harriet will be needing a nurse when she comes home from hospital . . .'

It was six weeks later when Jude and Sara drove home to Knight's Ferry. Jude had left his car at the airport when they flew off to Hawaii for their honeymoon three weeks ago, and now, after a stopover in London to recover from the flight, they were returning to the house. True to his word, Lord Hadley had given Jude a house on the estate, but contrary to his expectations it was not an old house, but a brand new one, at present being built to Jude's own specifications. Harriet had not been pleased about that. Knight's Ferry would eventually be Jude's, she said. What point was there in building another house? She had calmed down somewhat when Jude had pointed out that he hoped she would live for years and years, and that her grandchildren would need somewhere to stay if he and Sara had to go away. Now she was quite resigned to the marriage, and already planning her grandchildren's future.

'She may have a grandchild sooner than she thought,' murmured Sara rather ruefully, sliding her arm through Jude's sleeve and resting her head briefly on his shoulder.

'Yes.' Jude cast a searching look at her. 'How do you feel? You looked so pale before lunch.'

'Oh, I feel wonderful now,' Sara assured him smilingly. 'Maybe it was something I ate.'

'And if it wasn't?' he probed huskily. 'Do you mind?'

'Do you?'

'Me?' Jude's lazy eyes caressed her. 'Oh, love, how can I mind if you're having my baby, when we had so much pleasure putting it there.'

'Jude!' She pressed her fist into his ribs, and he grinned at her.

'Isn't it true?' he asked, teasing her deliberately. 'And me with the scars to prove it.'

Sara collapsed in giggles, but Jude had sobered, his eyes intent. 'Seriously, Sara, how do you feel about this? Have I been selfish? Do you wish we'd—well, taken some precautions?'

'I wouldn't have let you,' she declared fervently, sliding one arm around his neck and stroking the hair at his nape. 'Besides, I suspect if I am pregnant, the damage was done before we left for Hawaii.'

Jude gave her a rueful glance. 'And you don't mind?'

'Mind?' Sara raised her arms above her head, stretching luxuriously. 'Darling, I want your baby. It's part of you.' She turned to look at him. 'I love you, Jude. I don't know how I existed so long without you.'

'You shouldn't say things like that when we're on a motorway, travelling at seventy miles an hour, and I can't do anything about it,' Jude reproved her urgently. 'But when we get home——'

'We'll see how Laura has been coping,' declared Sara provocatively, smoothing her dress decorously over her knees, and meeting his frustration with wide laughing eyes.

Confirmation of Sara's pregnancy seemed certain a week later after several mornings of sickness. But awakening on

Saturday morning, to the delightful awareness of her husband's warm body still close beside hers in the wide bed, Sara was surprised to find Janet standing at the bedside, carrying a tray of tea and biscuits.

'Why, that's very kind of you, Janet,' she smiled, pulling herself up on the pillows and making sure to keep the thin sheet over her nakedness. 'But—lately——'

'I know,' Janet set the tray down on the bedside table as Jude stirred beside her. 'Ye've nae been stomaching your coffee. I've heard ye in the bathroom when I've been making the beds, and I've brought ye some tea and biscuits to put things right.'

'Oh, well. I—I don't know——'

Sara didn't ever feel sick until she got out of bed, and she was loath to increase the chances of her nausea, but Janet was determined.

'Try it, lassie,' she averred, making no move to leave her, and Jude opened his eyes enquiringly, as Sara obediently munched on a plain digestive.

'What time is it?' he groaned, reaching for his watch, but Janet forestalled him.

'It's after nine o'clock,' she declared firmly. 'And yon lassie's no putting a foot out of this bed until she's eaten these biscuits and drunk this tea.'

'Isn't she?' Jude viewed his wife with lazy adoring eyes. 'Well, I have no objections.' His mouth brushed Sara's smooth shoulder. 'Do you?'

Sara could feel her senses stirring in spite of Janet's severe presence, but she ate the biscuits and drank the tea, even though Jude refused the cup provided for him.

'Very guid.' Janet was satisfied when Sara was finished and picked up the tray. 'Ye'll have nae more trouble with this babby. Does Miss Ferrars know yet?'

Jude pushed himself into an upright position. 'No, she doesn't,' he said flatly. 'How did you find out?'

'Och, when a lassie starts bringing up her breakfast, and her not married three months, ye don't have to look far for the reason.'

Jude grimaced. 'I suppose you blame me.'

'Och, no.' For the first time Sara could remember Janet chuckled. 'She's a fine lassie. She'll hae no trouble. But don't you be pestering her, mind. She's got to rest.'

Jude grinned. 'Thank you, Janet.'

'Och, I'm leaving.' The old housekeeper made for the door. 'Ye'll be all right, missie. I'll see ye in a little bit.'

With the door closed behind her, Jude cast a thoughtful look at his wife and then got abruptly out of bed, walking across to the windows. Sara, surprised at his sudden detachment, followed him.

'What's the matter?' she asked, sliding her arms around him from behind, and pressing herself against him. 'Come back to bed.'

Jude bent his head. 'What Janet said—about you needing to rest—now that we seem to be sure——'

Sara pressed her lips against his shoulder blade. 'Don't be silly! Janet may have some good ideas—come to think of it, she has, I don't feel sick at all—but she's old-fashioned. And besides,' her hands strayed down over his flat stomach, 'if you think my condition means more to me than you do, you couldn't be more mistaken.'

Jude turned to her then, his eyes warm and gentle and disturbingly intent. 'Honey, I don't want to hurt you——'

'Then take me back to bed,' she breathed, her hands warm behind him, and with a groan of protest he acceded.

'I love you so much,' he muttered, after the urgency of their passion had been satiated. 'I can't leave you alone . . .'

'Just go on loving me,' murmured Sara huskily, and Jude answered: 'For the rest of my life . . .'

Harlequin Plus

A GRACIOUS ENGLISH TRADITION

Tea is "the sweetest dew of Heaven." So declared Lu Yü, a great Chinese connoisseur of the brew, more than a thousand years ago. Through the centuries, millions of people have agreed with him. It was primarily for tea that the European sailing clippers opened the route to China in the 1660s. In its early years in England tea was considered so valuable that it was sometimes sold in jewelry shops.

The English—and, incidentally, the Dutch and the Russians—took to tea as though they had been waiting for its advent all their lives. Samuel Pepys noted his first taste of "tee" in his famous diary in September 1660. Alexander Pope and other well-known poets gave it honorable mention in their writing. The amount of tea imported into the British Isles jumped from 143 pounds in 1669 to 63 million pounds in 1869.

Oddly enough, the English tradition of afternoon tea didn't begin until about 1840 when Anna Marie, Duchess of Bedford, popularized the custom—mainly because her family had shipping interests in tea!

But in spite of this leafy shrub's firm adoption by the West and its cultivation in such countries as India and Ceylon, the homeland of tea remains indisputably China. One or other of the two most common Chinese words for the drink, *ch'a* and *tay*, have gone into practically every language, from Russian and French to Swahili. In English both forms exist; in the British Isles the phrase "cuppa char" is as familiar as "cuppa tea."

We are sure Lu Yü would have been more than pleased at the worldwide acceptance of his favorite drink!